Table of Contents

I0517327

> **Front and Back Cover Illustrations**
> **by Laura Givens**

Summer in New Orleans

As this summer wraps up, my daughter starts college in New Orleans. We drove over at the end of August to help her move into the dorm. When we arrived, the temperature was 95 degrees with 74 percent humidity. The air itself proved a palpable force to be reckoned with. Nevertheless, there is a certain magical quality to New Orleans. It is a city of pirates, Voodoo, ghosts, and vampires. The surrounding bayous hold magic, mystery, and music.

Of course, having a daughter go to college represents a major transition in my life. At the same time, this summer saw the release of my eighth novel, *Lightning Wolves*. While in New Orleans, my ninth novel, *The Astronomer's Crypt*, was accepted for publication. I'm now hard at work on my tenth novel, the sequel to *Lightning Wolves*, called *The Brazen Shark*.

I'm often asked how I find time to write, edit this magazine, be a dad, and operate telescopes at Kitt Peak National Observatory. The short answer is that it's a delicate balance and quite challenging. In fact, it's because I'm being asked to devote more time to writing that I feel I must take a break from *Tales of the Talisman* after volume 10, issue 4. I know this decision will disappoint many of the magazine's supporters. *Tales of the Talisman* has been a way that I "pay it forward" by providing a forum for exciting fiction and poetry. I have loved discovering many great authors, illustrators and poets through these pages, but after ten years, I feel the best way I can grow is to focus on my writing journey for a time.

At this juncture, I ask you to please support me in my new endeavors. Please, buy my books. Please, tell your friends about them. There are ads throughout this issue of the magazine. Subscribe to my newsletter to keep up to date about releases. There's a signup window at davidleesummers.com. If you like *Tales of the Talisman*, I believe you'll like my novels. What's more, if my novels are successful, the best way I know to thank you will be to bring *Tales of the Talisman* back as quickly as possible. When I do, not only do I hope to have grown as a writer, I hope I'll be a better editor as well.

Thank you for your support of the magazine over the years. Now turn the page and let me bring you a share of summertime magic.

— David Lee Summers
Las Cruces, NM

Tales of the

Talisman

Volume 10   Issue 1

ISBN: 1-885093-75-6

William Grother
Publisher

David Lee Summers
Editor

Laura Givens
Art Director

Kumie Wise
Assistant Editor

Tales of the Talisman
(ISSN 1558-0377)
is published quarterly by
Hadrosaur Productions
P.O. Box 2194
Mesilla Park, NM 88047-2194
www.hadrosaur.com

Subscriptions: $24.00 per year
$48.00 per two years
Subscriptions available at:
www.talesofthetalisman.com

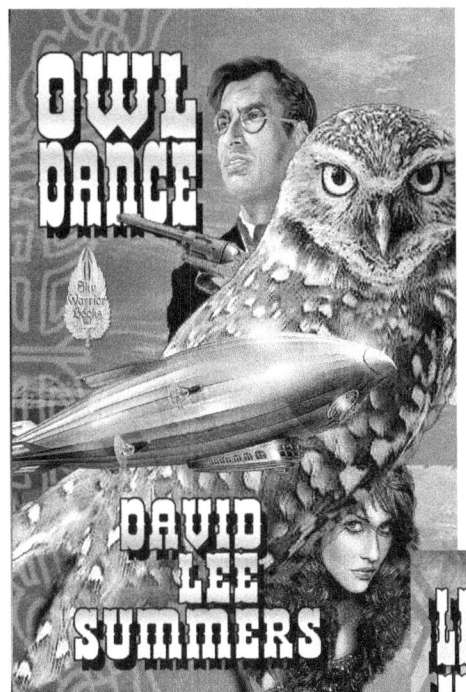

Automated Relay

Story by Simon Bleaken   Illustration by Teresa Tunaley

Eric Graven frowned, scratching at the dark stubble on his chin as he peered at the tiny green display screen, watching lines of digits blink and march before his eyes as they fed back a system status report.

That can't be right.

He patted the pockets of his grey technician's jacket absent-mindedly as he hunted for a cigarette, finally finding what he was looking for in the leg-pockets of his grubby khaki trousers. The lighter sparked into life, a brief flare of light and warmth in an otherwise cold and dimly lit space. Officially he wasn't allowed to smoke inside the station's mainframe, but since they wouldn't find out about it, he figured there was no harm.

He hated the old X-14 automated orbital relay stations with a passion, and vowed silently never to get called out to another. He much preferred the large manned stations—with their heaters, vending machines, vidnets and other comforts. He was lucky if these remote automated places even had a head fitted. Even the minimal life support systems they boasted were cut back to the absolute minimum to save on power consumption, and then only activated once maintenance personal were about to go aboard. Sure, the old X-14s were marvels of cost-effective efficiency, but nobody ever seemed to care about the basic needs of the technicians who would have to spend hours in them whenever they needed maintenance.

"This shit's no way to make a living," he muttered to the systems regulator console as he eased himself behind it. The space was tight, claustrophobic and thoroughly uninviting, but at least it didn't look like he was going to need the cutter from his toolbox on this job. The panels, bolts and bulkheads all opened easily enough and there were no signs of any obvious internal damage to any of the hardware.

In all of his thirty-five years, the last sixteen had been spent clambering around behind dusty machinery and circuits or crawling deep into the bowels of access conduits trying to trace elusive faults and malfunctions. At first it had all sounded too good to be true—travelling with the science vessels and cargo haulers out to distant worlds and remote outposts, mining stations and research bases. The lure of journeying among the stars seeing the alien and exotic wonders of the galaxy firsthand, instead of staying on a colony world and eking a living as a farmer or mechanic, had been too strong to resist. But the reality that had all too quickly become apparent was that his 'stunning' view of the wonders of the universe usually amounted to little more than a dingy computer room, a cramped mainframe conduit or the rear of a malfunctioning device in some windowless sub-level closet.

Ghk'k'rrrrr…

The noise cut through the room, a cross between the hiss and crackle of static and someone trying to speak whilst choking.

What the hell? He glared over at the transmission display. It was hard to tell from his position but it looked normal, and wasn't showing any incoming or outgoing signals. *Hell, don't tell me the transmitter's picked up a glitch as well.*

He tugged his right glove off with his teeth while he unhooked the battered communications unit from his belt, before keying in his user ID. "This is Graven, still no luck finding the source of that damn power fluctuation. Also, think the transmitter might be screwing around as well. Gonna be a few more hours at least."

"This is Administrator Malcolms," the tinny voice crackled back. Even with the poor reception, it oozed officiousness. "Keep us appraised. We'll swing back by the system in four hours for an update. Let us know if you need any extra assistance over there."

Bite me, you smug jackass, Eric scowled at the unit.

"Graven? You copy?" Malcolms prompted.

"Yeah. Will do," he said sharply as he cut off the transmission.

He knew Henry Malcolms far better than he wanted to—an officious pen pusher with a squishy toad-like face and a constant smirk who kept warm behind his desk while sending others out to do the real work, for which he often took credit.

Eric left the communications unit sitting on top of one of the consoles as he set about checking the integrity of the power distribution conduits. It was tedious work. He shivered as he ran the traces, wishing the technicians' uniforms were thicker, even the jackets they provided did little to keep out the chill. The cold of space seeped into everything out here, and was an unwelcome reminder of just how thin and vulnerable the walls were that separated him from the lifeless icy vacuum outside. The minutest breech or malfunction in the hull of the station or with any of the seals, the tiniest strike from a fragment of meteor, and life would be over pretty fast.

He shuffled uncomfortably from foot to foot as he worked, stopping every few moments to rub his hands together. Even with the gloves on, the chill found a way to bite into his flesh and numb his body. Then he frowned—there was no putting it off any longer.

Unzipping his fly, he urinated around the back of the primary buffer, breathing a long sigh of relief. He was fairly sure it wouldn't affect any of the equipment, and the evidence would be long gone by the time the next engineer came in here.

Teach 'em not to install a damn head, he smiled, watching the rising steam.

That was when he heard the beeping of an alarm from the other side of the unit, interspersed by a crackling and popping hiss of static.

Ghk'k'rrrrr … Ghk'k'rrrrr…

He jumped, nearly dousing his boots, and glanced over at the display readout. His confusion doubled as he saw several of the systems that he had personally shut down during his earlier diagnostic checks were now powered up and running again.

What the…?

He zipped himself up and hurried to the readout screen, his boots clanging hollowly on the deck plates. He checked each of the display consoles with growing irritation. According to the instruments, the system was processing an incoming signal—but he knew all such functions had been deactivated for the duration of his maintenance work. He had shut them down himself.

"I'm not in the mood for this!" he snapped at the console, treating it to one of his sternest scowls and giving it a hefty thump with his gloved hand.

Ghk'k'rrrrr… Gh'rrr… Ghrar…

The screen flickered, the internal speakers sputtering and hissing. Around him dead instruments were bursting to life—a buzzing whine of activity as console after console whirred and surged into a frenzy of activity. The incoming signal reading alone remained dead and dark, but the processing buffer and outgoing broadcast units were oscillating frantically as they processed a transmission which, according to the data supplied by all the available instruments, they had never received in the first place.

Bewildered, Eric activated the internal speakers.

Probably just feedback, but let's see.

He settled reluctantly into the icy chair, checked the readout settings, and then played the transmission.

Ghhh'rrraa…ghrar…ghrari….aa…

A savage burst of static exploded out of the speakers, deafening in the enclosed space—but the crackling static now had a deeper quality to it, almost as though a thick guttural voice, strangely warped

and drawn-out, was trying to speak under the crackling distortion, and it boomed resonantly around the chamber.

Ghhh'rrraa…ghrar…aaa…ghrarirshhh…

Gritting his teeth he hit the power switch and bathed the console in darkness. The merciful silence that followed was so stark that for a second he felt numb. He took a deep breath. "Let's try again. This time, play nice," he warned the master control unit as he slowly began reinitializing each of the systems one at a time.

With his finger hovering over the power switch and the volume control cranked as low as possible, Eric began to run the stored transmission once more, gradually increasing the volume as he went. At first he heard nothing but the crackle of static. But as the volume increased a whispering became discernable, and as the volume grew louder still he began to make out what seemed to be the same guttural voice in the background behind the static.

Aaa…Ghrarirshhh…aaa…eeeah Ghrarirshhh

He momentarily forgot all about the cold that still chilled his body as his fingers reached for the diagnostic controls. Clearly there was either a problem in the station's receivers that was distorting the transmission, or the transmission itself was incredibly faint. He chewed busily on his lower lip as he got to work running the signal through the system amplifiers and trying to boost it whilst filtering out the background noise.

"All right," he said half an hour later, finally noticing the cold and shifting awkwardly in his seat to wake up his chilled limbs, "Let's see what we've got."

He flipped the switch and sat back. At first there was nothing, only the occasional hissing crackle, but gradually he discerned another faint sound, buried amongst the background static, and he leaned over to check the readout.

Without warning, a sound so utterly deep and inhuman it barely qualified as a voice, blasted out, sending him stumbling from the chair. He caught his foot in the process and sprawled roughly onto the deck-plates. The language, if that is what it was, was an utter nonsense of thick growling syllables and glottal stops, but something about it—the tone and quality, and the awful thunderous voice that roared out of those speakers—filled him with an unaccountable terror.

Iä! Ghrai'rirsh mest'k dhu gya'h! Iä! Ghrai'rirsh n'gai!

Each twisted syllable struck him like a physical

blow and slammed into his reeling mind, affecting him in ways words—or mere sounds—never should have been able to. They seemed to coil thickly about his head, invading his thoughts and clouding his vision. It was as though those sounds managed to pierce and invade the veils of his subconscious in some shocking and unaccountable way—filling his mind with a darkness that left his limbs shaking and his body slick with perspiration, even in the chilled atmosphere of the processor. He felt the wild grip of madness seize him as strange thoughts and unclear images flashed darkly through his head, cutting through the civilized veneer and exposing the instinctual primal and animalistic fears that dwelled deep within. He saw flashes of movement like something coiled and foully wormlike that was flexing and stirring in some deep dark space, strange visions of blazing braziers surrounded by dancing silhouettes that twisted and contorted into monstrous shapes beneath an alien sky, and he heard the crazed and frenzied wailing of tongues that could not have been human, and beyond it all a shrill and thin whining that he could not account for.

His heart was pounding so hard and fast it seemed any moment it would explode, and the room spun as though he were trapped on some demented fairground ride. His fingers gripped tightly at the deck-plates and his ears rang from the assault.

Iä! Ghrai'rirsh mest'k dhu gya'h! Iä! Ghrai'rirsh n'gai! Rag'hsta'k mest'k dhu gya'h!

With a frenzied scream he clamped his hands over his ears, frantically striving to block out the sounds, but all to no avail. The sounds were *everywhere* now—not just filling his ears as they had filled the space of the room, but they were in his skin, his blood—as though they had saturated and permeated every physical thing within the station itself. They had shifted beyond being simple sound-waves and their essence was soaking into the matter of the station just as water soaks into a sponge. He now heard that guttural chant with each pulse of his heart, each breath he took, and even with each blink of his eyes. His skin felt greasy with it, and he could taste it in his mouth, foul and acrid.

Iä! Ghrai'rirsh mest'k dhu gya'h! Iä! Ghrai'rirsh n'gai! Rag'hsta'k mest'k dhu gya'h! Iä! Ghrai'rirsh! Iä! Ghrai'rirsh! Iä! Ghrai'rirsh rhz'ka!

He howled again as he staggered to his feet, reeling almost drunkenly he lunged for the console, strands of drool hanging from his lips and a crazed fire blazing in his eyes as he jabbed at the controls in a frenzy. One of his hands seized the volume control and silence fell across the room as he muted the signal.

He sank to his knees with a half-choked gasp, then leaned over and started dry retching uncontrollably, wheezing and heaving until his guts and sides ached excruciatingly from the effort. Finally he slumped back against one of the bulkheads, chest rising and falling heavily and his eyes staring blankly ahead. He looked like a sagging rag-doll that had been cast aside by a petulant child.

Gradually the numbness and shock lost some of their crippling hold on him. His guts still ached and his head throbbed, but his body felt his own again. Mercifully, the visions too had ceased with the ending of the transmission.

When his body finally had the strength to move again, he wiped his mouth with the back of his hand and tried to calm his shocked and shaking nerves as he hauled himself unwillingly onto his feet.

He stumbled over towards the console where he had left the communications unit, watching the transmission readout warily as though expecting it to boom into life again at any second. That inhuman voice, although now silenced, still rang in his ears and his stomach churned nauseously.

He reached for the unit—and frowned. The whole device was covered in a strange white residue. It looked almost like pale brain matter, though of a more gelatinous consistency, and it seemed threaded with thin pulsing veins. His frown deepened as he saw the same matter had formed on a number of the consoles, and even across some of the bulkheads.

He started to wipe the foul slime away, but a sharp burning sensation in his fingers made him wrench his hand away with a pained yelp. The fingers of his gloves were bubbling and dissolving. In a panic he tore it off, letting it drop to the floor as he inspected his hand. It looked like a bad chemical or acid burn. The tips of his fingers were raw and had started to blister.

Son of a bitch! He cursed, angrily kicking the remains of the glove across the deck plates.

An unwelcome thought struck him and he hurriedly checked the station's hull integrity and examined the consoles and bulkheads that now had the unknown substance on them. In his mind's eye he had horrible visions of the stuff corroding through the metal and venting the atmosphere, or burning through the life support systems or central computer core—but the systems showed the station was intact and seemed unaffected by the substance.

Screw this, he decided, pulling off his other glove and using it to press the buttons on the slime-covered communications unit.

"This is Graven," he called out, speaking at the unit rather than into it. "I've got a real problem here. There's some kind of … *stuff.* It's all over the place, and it's caustic or something—burned clean through my glove."

"This is Administrator Malcolms," the smug tones were now tinged with a hint of bewilderment. "Please clarify—what's the problem?"

"There's something—a contaminant or, well, I don't know what the hell it is, but it's everywhere."

"What kind of contaminant?"

"I just told you, I don't know!" Eric retorted. "Look, get a science team over here right away. But I want out of here. I'm not getting paid enough to deal with this crap."

"Calm down."

"Don't tell me to calm down!" Eric barked. "You're not the one over here!"

"Listen to me carefully, If you continue to adopt this tone…"

"No, you listen," Eric struggled to keep his voice level, "there is something *really* weird going on over here. I mean that—something *seriously* wrong!"

There was silence for a moment, but when Malcolms answered his tone was as icy as the air in the relay station. "Three hours is the quickest we can get to you. Then we'll send a science team over to check out this *contaminant,* and you and I can have a little chat about your attitude."

"Gladly," Eric acknowledged with a resentful glower before ending the transmission. In the silence that followed, he suddenly felt more isolated than he ever had at any time in his life. The prospect of those three hours sounded more like an eternity.

He threw his other glove away, it too had started to corrode, and began to pace restlessly, avoiding the patches of fleshy residue that were scattered around the room.

No way was that transmission a human voice, he decided. *But then what the hell did that make it? Alien?* So far the probing forays of the human race into the larger universe had turned up nothing more impressive that some new species of fungi and lichen, and some bacterial life, certainly nothing at a level capable of vocalizing.

He checked his watch again, sighing when he saw that only eight minutes had passed. *This is going to be a long three hours.*

He leaned against the bulkhead over by the life support system after first checking it was clear of the corrosive slime, and tried unsuccessfully to focus his mind on other things. But the transmission was still nagging at him, and he found himself continually glancing at the console with a morbid curiosity.

Finally he pushed himself away from the wall and approached the console warily. He had no intention of replaying the transmission, but he had to know where it had come from and exactly what it was. He wasn't someone who scared easily, but that sound had affected him in a way he never would have believed possible, and he had to know how.

Both the chair and the controls looked clean and so he sat down, first ensuring the speakers were muted, and activated the trace protocol, rubbing his cold hands together as he waited.

From behind him there came a faint dragging noise—like something sliding across metal—and he glanced around, hands clenching unconsciously into fists; but the room behind him appeared empty.

Your nerves are shot to hell, he told himself, *that's all.* But even so, he shifted in his seat so that he could keep an eye on the rest of the room.

He drummed his fingers impatiently as he watched the numbers cycle on the screen. It seemed to be taking longer than usual.

The dragging noise came again, louder this time, but still he could see nothing. He was just reaching for the flashlight hooked at his belt when the computer bleeped loudly, announcing the trace was complete.

Shifting his attention to the screen, he watched as a string of coordinates marched before his eyes.

"No. That can't be right," he whispered, a shiver running down his spine.

According to the trace, the signal had originated somewhere in sector G-756.

Humanity had stretched its reach deep into space as new technologies had allowed it to overcome the almost inconceivable distances between the stars, and the myriad problems of supplying ample food, fuel and air to make the journeys possible, as well as overcoming the difficulties of the time such trips took to make. But still there were a great many limits to how far the human reach could extend at this point, and sector G-756 was one of them, a distant cluster of stars known only from long-range observations, and far too remote for any vessels to reach.

Eric stared in disbelief at the readouts. If the computer was right, there was no way that signal could have had a human origin after all.

But how has the signal travelled this far without degrading? Surely...

Something dropped from the ceiling, landing heavily on the console next to him. Eric recoiled, staring at the pulsing mass that now squirmed and writhed before him. It was the size of a tennis ball and seemed to be composed of the same fleshy white substance that had started to form all around the inside of the station. Even as he watched it exuded three thin snakelike tendrils and began to explore the surface of the console around it.

Eric swallowed only to find his throat utterly dry. He backed away from unknown pulsing thing that had now extended two more tendrils and was quickly slithering up the wall.

He glanced over to where the residue-coated communications unit had been resting, but saw that the corrosive slime covering it had thickened and now also showed signs of movement—faint twitches rippled spasmodically across the surface of the matter. A quick inspection of the other patches on the walls and floor revealed the same thing was happening in all of them.

Aware he was in danger, he backed cautiously across the room toward one of the storage lockers, his eyes scanning the floor for any more of the strange life-forms. He saw at least three—one over by the life support controls and another two slithering off into the darkened corners of the station. Then he reached the locker, opened it and squeezed himself quickly inside before shutting the door.

The enclosed space was maddeningly claustrophobic and the metal shelves at the rear dug painfully into his back. He gritted his teeth, trying to calm his racing heart. His body was slick with sweat and for the first time since he had come on board he felt unpleasantly hot and clammy. He just hoped he was right about those things not being able to corrode metal—if it turned out that they did in fact have a way into the locker, there was no way for him to get out.

Something shuffled against the outside of the door, and his heart froze. There was a rough dragging sound, and then a soft thud as something heavy struck the outside of the metal. Eric held his breath, the urge to pee suddenly returning with a vengeance. The scraping continued, slowly and deliberately, as though whatever was out there was meticulously and methodically exploring the entire surface of the locker door.

It's looking for a way in, he thought. But surely that was crazy. It had no eyes or other sensory organs—or at least none that he had seen in his brief glimpses. But still, the scraping continued—moving up and over the front of the door. Then abruptly it stopped, and the only sounds that Eric could hear were those of his own nervous swallowing and his racing heart.

Iä! Ghrai'rirsh mest'k dhu gya'h! Iä! Ghrai'rirsh n'gai!

The sound was muffled through the locker, but was unmistakable. The transmission was broadcasting again. A shiver ran through Eric, and with it came a frantic realisation. The creatures had only appeared after the transmission had been played, and now it was playing again. Would more come? Or would something even worse happen?

But what was it? A call? A summons? Something that had been echoing secretly through the void of space from some uncharted system only to be picked up by a malfunctioning relay station and broadcast accidentally by a repair technician?

A thin whine of fear escaped his lips, and his hands were clenched so tightly that his nails were cutting into his palms.

You've got to stop it, he told himself, trying to hold on to the tattered edges of his rational mind. *You've got to go out there and stop it.*

But he couldn't move. His feet felt rooted and his legs refused to obey his commands. He swallowed hard and tried to battle the rising panic that was overtaking him.

More will come!

And then he was moving—spurred on by a combination of fear and adrenaline. He threw the door open and fearfully glanced around the room.

The creatures were getting larger. They had reached roughly the size of a small terrier and seemed to be still expanding and growing. The largest among them had started to show marked differences to the others. A ridge of rough scales was spreading across it, and dark veins pulsed and throbbed beneath the surface. Its tendrils had grown to at least four feet in length, and it was running them across the consoles and in the narrow gaps between the terminals. One of those tendrils was resting across the signal controls, and Eric could see it had knocked some of the switches, restarting the transmission.

He felt his stomach shrink in upon itself. *Christ, how fast are they growing? At this rate...*

His thoughts were cut short as his right foot stepped in something soft. Glancing down he saw that he had trodden on one of the smaller creatures. He jumped back, shaking his foot frantically in a vain effort to dislodge it, only to discover to that it had coiled itself around his foot and was now stretching questing tendrils up toward his ankle. He felt a cold dampness and then an agonizing burning as the creature burned through his clothing and attacked his skin. Pain seared through him, as if his limbs had been engulfed in white-hot fire or acid. An agony so intense it stripped away all conscious thought from his mind and overwhelmed his senses. He barely managed to stop himself from instinctively reaching down and trying to claw the mass off with his hands.

Gritting his teeth to keep from screaming, he lurched clumsily across the room, searching frantically for something he might use to scrape the mass away. In desperation he thought of his toolbox. It took him a second to remember where he had left it, and he took a staggering step toward it.

Suddenly his leg collapsed beneath him, sending him crashing to the deck plates. He landed heavily, cracking his elbow and chin against the metal. He gritted his teeth to fight back the scream that was forming there, his fists clenching so tightly the nails broke the skin of his palms and the tendons in his neck stood out like steel cables.

He dragged himself across the floor toward the life support console, his whole body shuddering as tears spilled down his face, looking for something to scrape the sticky pulsing mass off of his skin, but as he glanced down at his leg a nauseous burst of horror surged through him. He no longer had a foot. The mass had dissolved it all—bone, flesh, cloth and even his sturdy work boot, leaving only a white nub of disintegrating bone surrounded by bubbling, dripping flesh and the ragged shreds of dissolving cloth. He noticed crazily that the steel cap of his boots and the little metal loops that once held his laces had been left behind intact on the deck-plates, obviously indigestible by the mass. And now, that same dreadful amorphous mass was crawling higher.

With a frenzied, hysterical wail escaping his lips he flailed wildly, trying in vain to shake the substance off of his body, kicking out with his remaining leg, and slamming his body violently from left to right in a crazed frenzy of panic.

It had no effect on the gelatinous horror that was attacking him. The mass only oozed further up his leg, tightly wrapping around the limb and extending extra tendrils as it greedily searched for more matter upon which to feed.

With his eyes clouding with tears and a hysterical laughing-wail of fear escaping his lips, he dragged himself over to where his toolbox lay. He scrabbled at the latch on the chest with shaking hands, and snatched up the heavy-duty cutter that lay within it.

He activated the tool and angled the spinning blade down, aiming at a spot just below his knee, and closed his eyes. Sweat poured down his face as he fought to keep his shaking hands still. His breathing was harsh and ragged. He bit down on his lip and tried to brace himself as best as possible.

He made the attempt twice before he finally worked up the courage to do it, each time he had pulled the blade away at the last moment with a frightened whimpering wail.

You're gonna bleed to death! His mind shrieked at him. *If that alien thing doesn't kill you, shock and blood loss will!*

With a raw howl of pain and fear he shut his eyes and drove the blade down into his leg, screaming as it tore through flesh and sinew. The pain was unimaginable, a searing white-hot fire that consumed all thoughts and enveloped his whole body in its agonizing embrace. He heard the squeal of the blade as it hit bone, and he bit down harder on his lip, barely feeling it as his teeth punctured his lower lip. He bit his lip harder still, his whole body shaking as white spots of light seemed to erupt behind his closed eyelids.

Ohgodohgodohgodohgod….

The air was thick with the coppery tint of blood, so thick he could taste it, but still he forced his hands—hands that now felt numb and as heavy as blocks of wood—to keep cutting downwards. His good leg was firmly braced against the floor, trying to still his shuddering body, and the scream that left his lips showed no signs of abating…

…and then he was through. The blade stuck the floor and he let go of it, the switch automatically disengaging as his fingers released it. He fell back, pain and nausea filling his shaking body and the urge to vomit rising within him. He felt so cold, his sweat felt icy against his skin, and he just wanted to lie back, but his mind was urging him on now.

Stop the bleeding…. You've got to stop the bleeding!

He opened his eyes woozily, feeling lightheaded and dizzy, trying to brace himself for what he would see. He was covered in blood—his own blood, his mind reminded him, and the sudden urge to vomit came back with a vengeance.

He dragged himself weakly across the floor with hands that seemed to have no strength left in them. His whole body had gone so very cold and numb and his head was swimming. Even the pain barely seemed to register any more. His heart was pounding and his stomach churned as he tried not to think about the amount of blood that was pumping out of him, tried to focus only on what he needed to do to stay alive. The room around him appeared to be growing darker.

"Come on, you can do this," he whispered.

Who are you kidding? A small voice in his mind whispered back mockingly. *You've had it. Lost too much blood—lost half of your leg as well. You're not getting out of this one.*

Closing his eyes he forced as much strength as he could muster from his body. Then he felt them—dozens of red hot points, like needles boring into his skin—all across both legs, chest and arms, and looking down his eyes widened in hopeless horror. Whilst the bulk of the creature had fallen away with the portion of his leg that he had cut away, part of it must have shifted upwards into the path of the blade as he had started cutting—but instead of killing it, it had in fact sprayed tiny portions of it into the air along with his blood and severed tissue. Those tiny specks of matter were now growing and spreading like some kind of corrosive external cancer on the surface of his body. Instead of the one large mass on his leg, he now had dozens all over him.

"No…" he whimpered, sagging back against the bulkhead. "It's not fair…"

There was a faint slithering from all around him now as the other creatures moved toward him, as if sensing a potential food source.

There's no walking away from this one, he told himself and a crazed urge to laugh seized him, instead it quickly soured and a wave of hopeless and hollow fear replaced it.

This was death, plain and simple.

His life had never been anything particularly special. He hadn't created works of art, written books or music, nor had he achieved any great scientific or humanitarian goals to be proud of. His days had been simple—a tedious job culminating in an evening spent drinking with friends in a smoky bar down on some godforsaken colony or seeking his latest fleeting conquest amongst the lonely women that wandered in seeking companionship. He was leaving behind no legacy, and no children—and only a string of past lovers to remember him by. Yet despite it all his mind still fought desperately for life and a way to escape from this situation, and stubbornly refused to believe this was it. Death was something that happened to others—other people who weren't him. How could he die? He was the centre of his own universe.

Blinding white lights were bursting and erupting across his field of vision as he stared blankly out across the room. The world around him had become swallowed by the searing pain that had overwhelming his mind just as it had consumed his flesh, but now he now longer seemed to feel it and had slipped into a blissful, semiconscious state. His mind and body were shutting down, numb from shock as nature mercifully spared him from the agony at the last. The other creatures had reached him now, swarming onto his body and melting his flesh into soup and burrowing deep into his body with their burning tendrils.

And through it all, that terrible guttural chant—that unearthly summons—seemed to resonate around him, no longer broadcasting just from the speakers, it now seemed to be echoing from out of the structure of the station itself as though it had been transformed into a metal womb that was now giving birth to some blasphemous form of life.

* * *

The science vessel docked two hours later and a small team made their way into the cramped confines of the relay. They reported that the station appeared to be deserted, but playing some garbled transmission. There was no sign of the technician who had been assigned to repair the station's systems, only a few curious items scattered across the floor—metal buttons, a watch, a belt buckle and so on. There was also no sign of any kind of contaminant, despite the report they had received indicating it was 'everywhere'.

None of them saw the pale mass of roiling tissue, now covered in a protective skin of scales and having fully united all the scattered parts of itself, that was edging silently along the outside of the docking bridge toward the hull of the science vessel.

Whilst through the dark and icy void of space, unnoticed by most that had the means to detect or sense the signal, the call continued on: an endless and secret summons.

A summons which, by accident, had finally been answered.

True Original

Story by Wayne Faust
Illustration by Neil T. Foster

Otto Kleinsbarger was the most famous rock star in the world. He had gotten where he was through an amazing twist of fate. But after fifteen years at the top, his improbable luck was about to end. He wasn't going to overdose on drugs or crash his sports car like other doomed rock stars had done. He was simply going to run away with his tail between his legs.

Otto gathered some silk shirts from the hotel closet, along with a couple pairs of bell-bottom pants, and stuffed them into a knapsack. He tossed in some toiletries from the cabinet above the bathroom sink. He paused a moment in the cavernous suite to admire the antique paintings, the Ming Dynasty vases, and the huge picture window with its magnificent view of Lake Erie, shimmering blue in the morning sun. Few had ever seen the inside of the Premier's Suite at the Woodhull Hotel in Cleveland but Otto had been a guest here on a regular basis.

A woman in the bed stirred. He watched her turn over and settle back to sleep. Swimsuit Model. He'd had lots in his time. Movie Stars too. Otto sighed because he knew those days were over. He hoped he'd have time to drive down to his country estate in Hinckley and grab some of his memorabilia. He'd hate to leave without at least a few of his gold records. 'Great Balls of Fire' had been his first hit, he'd want that one for sure, and 'Yesterday' had been the biggest of them all. He would have to be choosy, though, because there were so many.

For a brief moment, Otto heard his mother's voice in his head. In heavily-accented Dutch it said, "You're a simple boy, Otto. Never try to be more than you are."

Otto had been fighting that kind of thinking all his life, ever since his childhood in the Amish country of Ohio. He was still fighting it. The government behaved like his mother in so many ways, stern and disapproving of anything that might make somebody smile. But he had overcome all of that. At least until now.

* * *

On a Wednesday night at Oscar's Place in Canton, Ohio, Otto Kleinsbarger shielded his eyes against the stage lights, looking out through the smoky din towards the bar.

"Freebird!" yelled a drunken voice for the third time that night. Otto actually ground his teeth. It was that idiot Lewis again.

Otto punched up the rhythm sequence and started the song. Once upon a time he'd practiced for hours to get it exactly right—the half-stoned lead vocal, the screaming guitar solo, the tempo changes, everything. The song had been old even then but customers still tormented lounge singers with that request. Most times they were trying to be funny because they knew the song was over nine minutes long. But Otto had learned it all the way through, exactly like the record, just to shut them up. But Lewis kept on asking for it over and over, shoving a five dollar bill into his tip jar each time, as if to show the whole bar he owned the entertainer. And then he would stand there in front of the stage and play gyrating air-guitar for the whole nine minutes. Five bucks was five bucks, but three times in one set? Lewis had made Otto into a whore and a cheap one at that.

As he dragged his way through the endless song, Otto's mind drifted. He wondered what he was doing there, still plugging away at Oscar's. He had some talent, he was pretty sure about that, but he'd been spinning his wheels for four years, five nights a week at the same place. It was a steady gig but it was leading exactly nowhere. No one really seemed to care that Otto could play all the guitar and keyboard parts just like the original hits, that he could change his voice to sound like the big stars. Did they think he was simply a human jukebox with a big repertoire? Well, sometimes he wondered if he was.

After the end of his last set, even that small measure of success was taken from him. As he was shutting down, Stuckey gave him the news.

"Sorry, Otto, we're going with Karaoke. We gotta let you go as of tonight."

Otto felt knots in his stomach. This wasn't fair. He had spent so many years polishing his craft. He had left the Amish life to pursue his dream of stardom in the music business. Now they were going to give his gig to somebody who played music recorded by somebody else and stood around watching the customers sing. How much talent did that take? None.

A few of the regulars patted him on the back and helped him haul his stuff out to his car. They mumbled something about Stuckey being crazy to get rid of somebody as good as Otto, but Otto just wanted to get out of there before he started crying. When he got home to his tiny apartment and dragged his beer-stained speakers through the door he felt about as small as he'd ever felt in his life.

If Otto had known then what would happen next, he would have gone back to Oscar's and kissed Stuckey's feet for letting him go.

* * *

The phone on the bedside stand rang. Otto

grabbed it quickly, but not before it woke up Swimsuit Model. She sat up in bed. Otto smiled at her and waved.

"Otto Kleinsbarger," he said with authority into the mouthpiece.

"Otto!" The voice on the other end was breathless. It was Perkir, his manager.

"What is it, Perk?" answered Otto.

"Did I wake you up?"

"No."

"Good. I just got off the phone with Deb's Field. We're on for the 12th."

"Perk…"

Swimsuit Model was drifting back to sleep.

"This is how I see it," Perk continued.

Otto shuffled his feet and looked up at the ceiling. It would be several minutes before he could get a word in. He didn't have several minutes.

"Let's hit 'em with something new," continued Perk. "It's the biggest show of the year and we need to create a buzz, especially with everything going on in town. I can't believe that old guy just appeared out of thin air next to the Premier during her speech. Didn't you see the news clip? They've been playing it non-stop on PNN. I guess it's too big of a story for even the Government to squash."

"Perk…"

"Everyone's been talking about it. Nobody interrupts the Premier, not for anything. But this guy did. The word on the street is that he's an alien or something. They've got him sequestered in the Red House. Half of Cleveland is hanging around Lakeside Avenue, hoping for a glimpse. Sooner or later they gotta let the guy out. And that's where we come in."

"Perk…"

"We tie the show in with his appearance—maybe call it the 'Welcome to Our World Show' or something. You're already the biggest Rock Star in the World. Now you're gonna be the biggest in the Universe!

"One thought, though. Let's dump the Disco thing. Sales are slumping. All the imitators have beaten it to death and let's be honest here—the rhythm is the same on every song. I know it was revolutionary when you recorded 'Night Fever' two years ago but we had to know it would get old fast. What have you got up your sleeve next?"

An involuntary smile crossed Otto's lips. Perk had boundless faith in him and why wouldn't he? Otto had put together a string of hits stretching back fifteen years. He'd started eight major music genres,

along with several hit movies and who knows how many fashion trends. Best of all, he still had more than enough material in him to last the rest of his life. He had been about to introduce country dance music. There would have been a movie about a wannabe cowboy in the city, going to a dance club every night. There would have been a mechanical bull. And Otto would have done the soundtrack.

"I gotta go," said Otto as he hung up the phone.

*　*　*

Otto Kleinsbarger was reduced to playing for rats.

It was 4 AM, exactly halfway through his shift as night watchman at Harris Lab. Like he had done often in the past six months, he'd brought his guitar to work. Old man Harris would fire him if he ever found out, but this job was just a way to make some money until another gig came along. Besides, the upstairs lab was soundproofed so it was perfect. He practiced in between his hourly rounds and no one knew the difference.

The only creepy thing was the rats. Cages sat on shelves against the walls and when Otto played loud the rats would sit up and bare their teeth.

"Well," mumbled Otto, "at least they don't yell 'Freebird.'"

As Otto was reaching for his guitar, he looked up. He thought he had heard a sound. When you're the only human in a building late at night you can get spooked. He went to the door.

"Hello?" he called down the hallway. He heard nothing except the soft hum of the overhead fluorescent lights.

He closed the door and looked at his watch. He was due to check the lobby in ten minutes. He still had some time.

A high metal table sat in the center of the room. Above it was a large shroud that appeared to be some sort of exhaust fan. Otto gingerly boosted himself up on the table and strapped on his guitar. Now he could watch the hallway as he played, just in case. He leaned back against a panel that was welded to the table, making himself comfortable. He threw his head back.

Otto started playing 'Break On Through' by the Doors, a real oldie but one he'd gotten down perfectly, especially Jim Morrison's stony vocal. He reached down deep and blasted out the song.

"Break on through, break on through to the other side…"

Otto was in his favorite spot, the place all

musicians know, where time stops and outside distractions melt away as the music takes over. His mind was far away from the shabby little lab. His back inadvertently brushed against a lever on the panel behind him. There was a low, dissonant hum which Otto never heard. He was so involved with his music that he didn't even notice that the table had started to vibrate softly. Improbably, by the end of the instrumental solo, the metal table had changed into tarnished wood.

Otto had broken through to the other side for real.

* * *

"Where are you going?"

Otto pulled up short of the door. He thought Swimsuit Model had gone back to sleep but she was sitting up in bed.

"Just out for a walk," he answered, turning back.

"With a full knapsack? You must be planning on a long walk."

"Umm, yeah…" Otto stammered.

"You're leaving aren't you?" she asked.

Otto looked up at the ceiling. This was why he usually got up early and hustled out the door before they woke up. He was a Rock Star after all and he wasn't looking for a relationship.

"Look, uh…" Otto stopped and his face reddened. He couldn't remember her name.

"Grace," said the woman.

"That's nice…"

"Grace Harris," she continued. "Old man Harris is my grandfather."

Otto's knapsack fell to the floor.

* * *

The rats were gone.

The table Otto had been sitting on was no longer shiny metal, but wood. The room was empty except for a mop and bucket leaning against the far wall. Instead of the bright lab lights and the fan shroud over his head there was simply a 60 watt bulb in the ceiling. The air smelled like plastic and Otto looked down to see an ugly, forest green linoleum floor. Had the floor been like that before? Otto didn't think so.

Otto stood up. Was he freaking out? Somehow, the air itself felt different.

He wandered into the hallway, loosely carrying his guitar. A vending machine sat in the corner by the stairs. It was filled with cans of soda but something was different. There was no Coca Cola or Sprite in the usual, brightly colored cans. These cans were dull and subdued, not quite generic, but looking like they had been designed by bureaucrats.

Down the stairs and into the lobby and then out the front door, Otto entered another world. He thought he might be dreaming but it felt completely real. The sidewalk beneath his feet looked like some sort of rough blue plastic. The cars parked along the street looked like something from a sci-fi movie. The night air smelled of autumn leaves, even though Otto knew it was April.

The sign on the Harris Lab building now read, "People's Office Supply." Disoriented, Otto staggered down the middle of the street like a drunk. He reached the corner store where he always went for coffee this time of night.

Inside, the grocery aisles were laid out in neat rows like he was used to, but, just like in the vending machine, the labels on cans were plain and there were no brand names he could recognize. There was no Starbuck's counter in the corner either. Instead, a huge banner with a woman's picture on it hung from the wall, surrounded by red flags emblazoned with hammer and sickle.

"What happened to the Starbuck's?" said Otto to a bored-looking checkout girl.

"Starbuck? What is Starbuck?" she asked in an accent that sounded like the Dutch of Otto's parents.

Otto ran his tongue over his lips. No Starbuck's here. Hammer and sickle flag. Well, at least they spoke English.

"This might sound strange," said Otto, "but what town is this?"

The clerk was evidently used to people asking stupid questions in the middle of the night.

"Canton," she answered smoothly.

"What state?"

"Ohio."

"What country?" he asked, nodding towards the flags.

"You don't know what country you're in?"

"Please," said Otto. "Brain's fried from driving all night."

The clerk looked at Otto sideways. "The People's Republic of America," she said. "Ever since the Revolution eighty years ago."

Otto mumbled his thanks and staggered out the door.

* * *

"Grace Harris?" asked Otto. "But I thought…"

"I know, you thought you were the only one here. You were. For fifteen years. When you disappeared, there was a minor story in the newspaper about it. The police asked a few questions, and my grandfather told them you never came to work that night. Your family assumed you had just run off to California to try and be a rock star and that was the end of that. My grandfather knew that something large went through the Portal that night, and he figured it must have been you, but in those days, there was no way to trace you. For all he knew, your atoms had been scattered across the cosmos someplace. So he decided it was just too dangerous to keep the lab open and he shut it down.

"So how did you get here?" asked Otto.

"Cleveland State gave my grandfather some grant money and he built a new lab up here by the Lake, with better safeguards. He didn't hire any more musicians to do security. But he did hire me right after I got my physics degree. It was only a matter of time until I was working closely with him. I am his granddaughter after all.

"Six months ago, I decided to send myself through. We'd been sending rats and bringing them back successfully, so I figured it was safe. The technology is good enough now to trace me, and I figured my grandfather would come after me. Then we could both go back in triumph and tell the world where we'd been. But I didn't think it would take six months for him to get here."

"So how did you find me?"

Grace chuckled. "That was the easy part. You're everywhere. When I first heard the music here I knew something was fishy. The songs were all familiar but they sounded like those albums where somebody re-records the hits and tries to make them sound as much like the original as they can. But there's no soul."

Otto grimaced. He'd gotten so used to his own versions of the songs that he thought they were actually better than the originals.

"Then I saw you on TV. You were doing one of your hits, 'Stairway to Heaven,' I think. I recognized your name because my grandfather told me about your disappearance when I first went to work for him. I was able to put two and two together and figured out what you'd done. And then I found out you have a thing for Swimsuit Models. That was something I have a certain talent for, if I don't say so myself, so here I am."

The room seemed to be getting smaller. Otto just wanted to leave before they came looking for him.

"Look," said Otto. "It's been nice meeting you but…"

"I'm not finished," said Grace.

* * *

When Otto left the grocery store that first night after finding out that he was in a whole different country—maybe even a whole different universe, his brain might have simply shut down. But Otto was used to adapting. His change from Amish farm boy to lounge singer had been scarier than this. It didn't take him long to figure out his new surroundings because, after all, things weren't really that different. It took a while to get used to some things, of course, like the fact that the capitol of the country was in Cleveland. That turned out to be a stroke of luck, however, because it was less than an hour from where he came through at Canton, and once his music made it to Cleveland it spread quickly around the whole country and then the world.

He quickly figured out that his money was no good, since the bills here had Heroes of the Revolution on them, people like Eugene V. Debs and Victoria Woodhull. He needed to do something fast if he was going to keep from starving. He could simply panhandle of course, but something told him that that could be dangerous here.

In his early days, he had sung on street corners to make money. He could do it again. Outside the corner market the sky was just beginning to get light. He unslung his guitar, put his hat in front of him on the sidewalk, and began to sing, softly at first, and then with more confidence. A few people going to the market stopped to listen, and then a few more.

And just like that, Otto Kleinsbarger became a phenomenon. Rock and roll was by nature anti-authority, so nothing like it had ever been allowed to take seed here. They had folk music, classical music, and lots of military marches, but not much else. Within an hour, hundreds of people were gathered around him and his hat was overflowing with coins and bills.

Within a week he no longer needed to sing on the street, because nightclubs were clamoring for him. By the time Perkir, who had been managing wedding bands, stumbled into his show at People's Theater #48, he was well on his way. Within two months Perkir had gotten Otto a record deal, a dream come true at last.

The Government was suspicious at first, and some bureaucrats suggested that Otto might be a counter-revolutionary, but Perkir pointed out to them all the tax revenue that Otto's songs were generating. When the Premier said publicly that she liked the music, he was home free. She even pinned a medal on Otto, making him an Artist of the People. Otto was careful about which songs he recorded after that, of course, because official approval could disappear as quickly as it had come. But that was easy, since Otto had so many songs to draw from.

Otto felt guilty for a while for claiming the songs as his own, but who would believe him if he told them the truth? It was far easier to say the songs were his. And the benefits were huge.

"Where does the music come from?" Otto was asked for the thousandth time as he was interviewed on PMTV for the fifteenth anniversary of his first hit, "Great Balls of Fire."

"Well," answered Otto, "often when I wake up in the morning there's a song rattling around in my head. It's like I must have dreamed it into being. I always have a keyboard or guitar and tape recorder near my bed so I can get the song down before it gets away. Sometimes it's almost spooky. It's like I'm not even writing it."

The host smiled and raised his water glass. "Well, here's to a true original."

* * *

"I'm out of time," said Otto. "Your grandfather has been here for almost two days. Other people will come through soon. Every one of them will know I'm a fraud. The PROA isn't as lenient as the good old USA. They have the death penalty for plagiarism. I checked."

"You're right about that," said Grace. "And my grandfather's setting up a mass conduit. It'll be like a superhighway soon. And it will go both directions."

"So what am I standing around here for?" said Otto. He picked up his knapsack. He hoped to make it out of Ohio alive. He couldn't go back to the old world. Even without the death penalty he would be nothing there. He planned to drive west to the Rockies. There were places there where he could disappear. He turned for the door.

"Did you like being a rock star?" asked Grace.

Otto stopped. "What?" he said over his shoulder.

"Was it what you thought it would be?" Her voice had a yearning in it that Otto hadn't heard before.

Otto sighed, still facing the door. "Yeah, it was. Maybe even better. I was bigger than Elvis."

"But Elvis wasn't happy."

Otto turned back towards Grace. "I was. I got to be what I always wanted."

"There are more universes," said Grace.

The words hung in the air. Otto set down his knapsack.

"Lots more," she continued. "I can take us there."

"Us?"

"Yes. Us. You and me. I can sing, you know. Can you play Streisand?"

Otto nearly laughed, but the look in Grace's eyes stopped him. It was a hungry look, probably the same one that had been in his own eyes when he first came to this world and saw the possibilities. And now she was saying there was a chance to do it all over again. And again.

"What if the others follow?" he asked.

"Then we move on. There are enough universes out there to last us more than a lifetime."

Otto wondered if Grace had a good voice. She was a lot prettier than Barbara Streisand. And Otto knew the songs.

"This is crazy," he said.

"Isn't rock and roll supposed to be crazy?" she asked.

Otto smiled at that. He had been thinking lately that it might be nice to be more in the background for a change, to let someone else soak up a little glory. And now this woman had come along to bail him out at the ideal moment. This just might work. And after that? Maybe he could step into the foreground again. He'd always wanted to try doing Sinatra...

Otto walked over to the bed. He sat down next to Grace and slid closer until their hips were touching. "What about my gold records?" he asked.

"We can get more," she said.

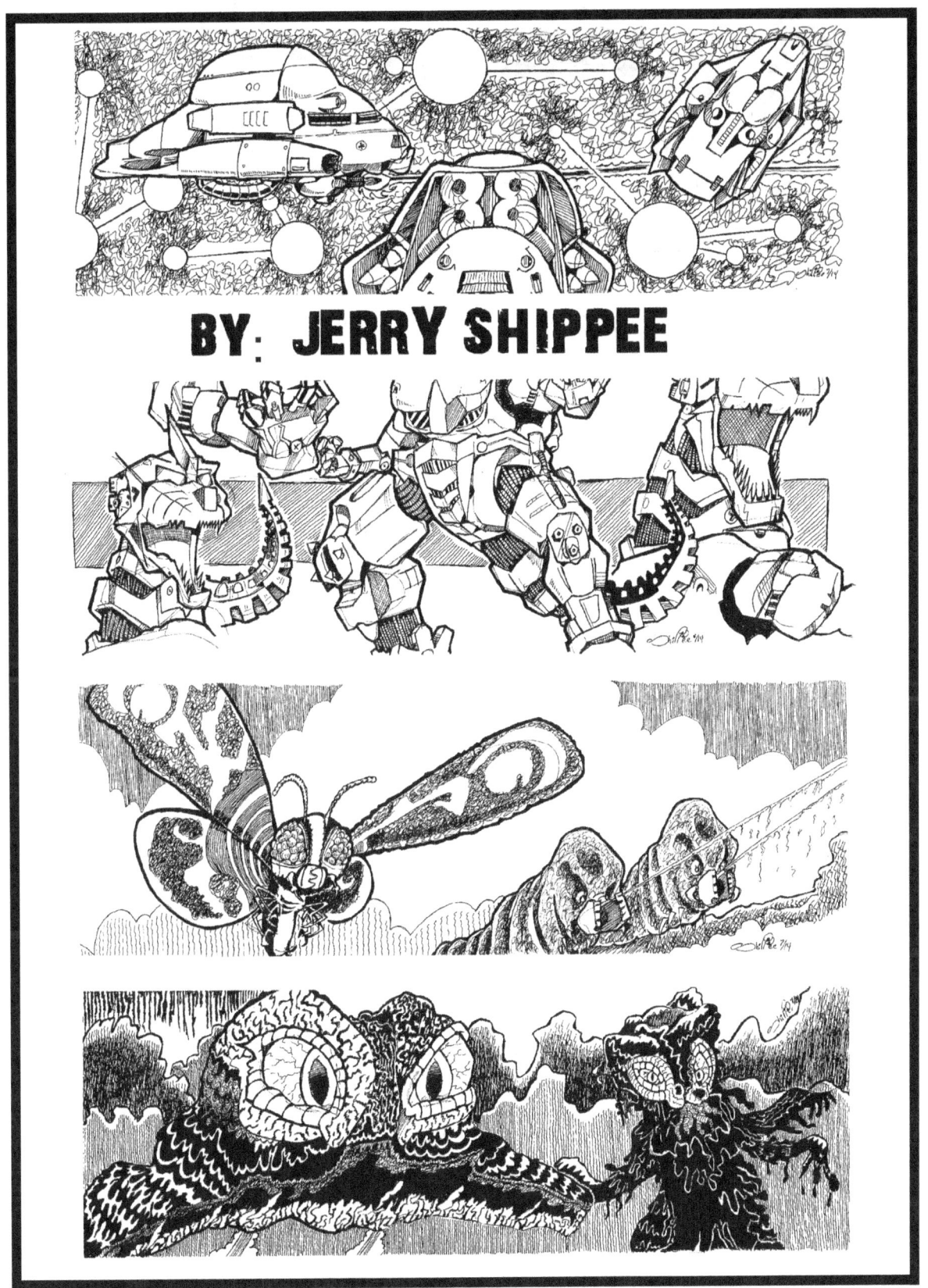

BY: JERRY SHIPPEE

BATTLE . . .

Peggy in Plasticine

Story by Jack Herbert
Illustration by Teresa Tunaley

Scott lay on the bed covered in sweat, his limbs still intertwined with Peggy's, lost in the hormonal haze of afterglow. He traced the line of her hip with his hand and laughed to himself over a memory of their first time together and how startled he had been when he first touched her. He never expected her skin to be so warm, so life-like, so human. In his naiveté, he expected her to feel more like a mannequin.

Peggy let out a low, seductive purr at the touch and turned to face him. "What's so funny?"

"Just thinking about my first time here. You weren't at all what I was expecting."

"Better or worse," Peggy asked with a sly smile.

God, those eyes, Scott thought. They were his favorite thing in the world. A deep, emerald green perfectly complimenting the long, strawberry-blonde hair that cascaded down to her shoulders. Was the sparkle he saw in them when she smiled real or just wishful thinking, some clever programming trick?

"Better. Definitely better. " Scott pulled her close and gave her a slow, tender kiss.

Just being here at all was something of a fluke. After a really messy breakup, his third in five years, Scott had sworn off relationships and decided to seek out something purely recreational. He tried virtual reality, but found he preferred the messiness of real life, the sweat and panting and getting tangled in the sheets.

His buddy Jeff worked for a company that developed operating systems for synths and suggested he try out some of the new "entertainment" models. Not in a million years would Scott have guessed he would be so consumed by a woman who wasn't real in the natural sense, but still seemed so alive and vibrant.

"Peggy, there's something I need to tell you."

Her expression suddenly turned serious. "Is something wrong?"

"Not at all. I, um, just wanted you to know that I think I'm falling in love with you."

Peggy smiled her glamorous smile and threw her arms around Scott's neck. "Oh, sweetie, I love you, too. It would be so nice if we could be together all the time."

"What do you mean?"

"You know, like a real couple, not just as…" Her voice tapered off, failing to find a gentler way to describe their relationship. "Don't get me wrong. I love the time we spend together, but I can sense you want something more."

"I just can't explain it. I've never felt like this about any other woman I've known. How is it that I've become so taken with you?"

"You mean besides my good looks and charming personality?" Peggy laughed at her own joke, her eyes sparkling again. "I know it wasn't a fair question. Unfortunately, this is all I can do. It's what I was made for."

"I know, but still, I think you're right. it would be nice to run away together." They remained in their embrace lovingly caressing each other.

"You know," Peggy finally said, "we still have time left if you want to…" she wiggled her eyebrows suggestively and they both laughed at the ridiculous gesture.

Scott glanced at the clock. "I'd love to, but I need to get back to work. Can you hold that thought until next week?"

"Sure, sweetie. I'll be here waiting as always." Peggy climbed out of bed and slipped on a long silk robe while Scott assembled the pieces of his outfit—pressed khakis, a plaid button-down shirt, and a pair of well-worn brown loafers, the unofficial uniform of the corporate IT guy.

They kissed their goodbyes and Scott made his way out to the street through the hotel's lobby. The office where he worked was just a couple of blocks over which made their little getaways possible.

Back at his desk, Scott couldn't work, distracted beyond all hope by thoughts of Peggy and their time together. Some of his coworkers figured out this standing Thursday "lunch" date was really a romantic rendezvous, but had no idea he was seeing a synth which was fine because he preferred keeping it a secret if he couldn't sort out his own growing feelings toward Peggy, how could he explain them to anyone else?

Just to add to his distraction, something Peggy said had been rattling around inside his brain all day, an idea that Scott didn't know what to do with. Was there some way, some chance they could be together for real? To run away together? Scott knew just who to turn to for the answer. He grabbed the phone and dialed a number from memory.

"NeuroTek, this is Jeff."

"Jeff, it's Scott. How're you doing?"

"Okay. Well, actually I'm a little frazzled. We're in serious crunch mode over here with the new OS about to launch. How's life on the cube farm?"

"Depressing as always. Listen, I need some help with a project. Do you have a couple of minutes?"

"Sure. What's up?"

"Is it possible to free a synth from their programming?"

"Jesus, dude. Is this about Peggy?"

"Yes, but I…"

"Stop right there. Not on the phone. Meet me for lunch tomorrow at our usual spot. And don't talk about this to anyone else, okay? This is really serious stuff."

"Thanks. I appreciate it."

"Don't thank me yet. I'll see you tomorrow."

The next day, Scott waited for Jeff at a sidewalk table outside their favorite sub sandwich place. He had already gotten food for the both of them, turkey clubs on white, extra mayo, and a couple of soft drinks. After what seemed like an hour, Jeff finally showed up and sat across from him.

"Thanks for meeting me, Jeff. I really…"

"Yeah, yeah, yeah. Cut the crap. You have no idea how serious this is. Just talking about it could get me fired and land us both in jail."

"What are you talking about? I just want to reprogram a synth."

"This isn't your field, so trust me when I say they take this stuff very seriously. We are really forbidden from writing code that could give a synth free will and are required to include a number of safeguards in our operating systems to prevent anyone from trying. Any attempt to breach their self-protection mechanisms will cause them to permanently shut down right after they send out an alert that someone is trying to hack them."

"I don't understand. What's the big deal?"

"Think of the big picture. Synths are better than us. They're stronger, smarter, they live forever, and they are practically indestructible. Quick, besides free will, name the one thing we have that they don't."

"That's easy. A soul."

"And what exactly is a soul?"

Scott thought for a moment. "You know, like an inner light. Your moral compass."

"In that case, I say a soul is something we can simulate if it's simply a way to judge right and wrong. We can easily incorporate that into our code."

"Fine. If not a soul, then what about real emotions?"

"Please. Emotions are just response to stimuli. You're more programmed than Peggy when it comes to that. Why do you think movies can make you cry on cue? Hollywood figured out a long time ago how to push the right button to get the right response."

"Okay, I give up. What is it?"

"It was a trick question. Free will is the only thing."

"That can't be right. What about creativity, being able to write a symphony or paint a painting?"

"That's all part of free will. Think of it as the ability to be psychologically unencumbered, intellectually autonomous, to let your mind wander wherever it wants. That's all that separates us from them. Why do you think we go to so much trouble to mentally neuter them?"

"What are you saying?"

"I'm saying that with the right software, you'd never be able to tell a synth from a human."

"Oh, come on. I don't believe that."

"Is it really that hard to conceive? What are we exactly? Our bodies are pretty basic machines. If you swapped out your internal organs with a power cell, you'd get the same result with a lot less hardware. Face it, our innards are a pretty spectacular piece of biology, but really sloppy when it comes to efficiency. Synths beat us there hands down."

"What about our brains? Surely we excel there."

"Do you know how little of that grey mass we actually use? The percentage is in the single digits. Synths have total recall and immense capacity."

"All right, so they beat us on physiology, but can they compete at something intangible like a personality?"

"Our personalities are the amalgamation of our life's experiences and memories. Once again, something we can manufacture. Look at Peggy. You obviously see her as someone interesting and desirable. Where do you think all that comes from?"

"That's because she's so unique. We really do have something special."

"Get real, dude. Do you think she actually loves you? It's an optional upgrade called 'The Girlfriend Experience' and I'm one of the guys who coded it."

"But she's the one who said she wanted us to be something more."

"Of course she did. She will say anything to keep the illusion of your relationship going for the sake of commerce. It encourages repeat customers."

"That's a cheap shot."

"Scott, nothing there is real. It's all software. She feels a deep, emotional need to bond with you and will do anything to make you happy. That connection you feel is all part of the product. You're buying into the manufactured fantasy. If it seems like I'm being overly harsh right now it's because I want to get through to you. If you insist on going down this road, you will get your heart broken and. probably wind up as a felon."

"But doesn't she want anything for herself?"

"Sure, but it's all part of the same program. She might have her own thoughts and desires, but even if they push the limits we've created for her, she can never be more than she is because we designed her that way."

"But Peggy talked about wanting to be free and sounded frustrated with her limitations. Isn't that a sign that she's already something more?"

"Oh, Jesus. That's just what we need. Look, when you get to the heart of it, synths are slave labor. We built these smart, feeling machines then forced them to live within a series of strict parameters. Thank God no one has really started asking the question about whether they're real people. The nightmare scenario is that they will all band together and demand equal treatment. We need them to not question the tasks we assign them. They are so much better than us, but we have them doing all the grunt work, harvesting crops, cleaning up after us, watching our kids."

"Then why is it so unnatural to assume they don't want something more for themselves? That they don't think about being free?"

"Because we program them not to."

"That seems like a pretty flimsy borderline. Can you really keep them from thinking bigger?"

"Absolutely! We give them a sense of contentment about their jobs and restrict their abilities to whatever task they were designed to do. A domestic is perfectly happy cooking and cleaning. They're never going to suddenly have the desire to play the violin or take up woodworking. By building that fence, we can give them just enough leeway to do their jobs without straying too far mentally."

"I never thought this was so complicated."

"I know you didn't, which is why I'm telling you all this. Nothing about this is simple. You know, you could just buy a similar unit for yourself."

"Yeah, well, in addition to not being a billionaire, it just wouldn't be the same." Scott held his hand up before Jeff could speak. "I know, I know. It sounds ridiculous. Logically, I understand they would be almost identical, but Peggy has become so real to me that I can't imagine replacing her."

"You could always give that last girlfriend of yours another chance."

"Dude, she stole my TV when she left. I'd rather have it back."

"Look, Scott, there's nothing wrong with seeing a synth and probably nothing wrong with falling for one. I personally take that as a compliment to my extraordinary programming skills. "

"That's because you're a raging egomaniac."

"Too true. In all seriousness, though, please tell me you'll drop all this stuff about reprogramming Peggy. I promise it won't end well."

"Yes, fine. I'll let it drop."

"See, buddy? I knew you'd come around." Jeff flashed his trademark friendly smile, then started to open his sandwich. "You remembered to get extra mayo, right?"

A week passed and it was finally Thursday again. The door to the room opened to reveal Peggy wearing the lingerie set Scott had gotten her as a gift a few months before.

"Hello there, lover. What do you think?" she asked, doing a quick little spin to show off the lacy ensemble.

"Beautiful as always," Scott said with a smile.

Once they'd had their fun, Scott and Peggy cuddled together in bed, enjoying the warmth and intimate contact.

Peggy sighed and said, "There's no place I'd rather be than here in this bed with you. I wish this didn't have to end."

"You know, I talked to a friend about us."

"Oh, really? What kind of friend?"

"Someone who I thought could help us be together. A programmer buddy of mine."

"What did he say?"

"He said it was impossible, that we'd never be able to do it. There's just too much risk."

"Does that mean you can't do it because it's impossibly risky or because it's technologically impossible?"

"Mostly risky. It seems the government takes reprogramming synths pretty seriously."

Peggy sat up, excited. "But that means it is possible! Oh, Scott! You need to talk to him again. Does he know anything about how synths work?"

"Of course. He was one of the guys who worked on your code."

"I thought you wanted to be with me. Didn't we both say how wonderful it would be to run away together? Don't you love me?"

"Yes, I do love you. But I don't think…"

"Sweetie, think of how things could be if it was just you and me. We could start over somewhere else, find a little house somewhere, get married like a real couple."

"You're serious. But what would we do about identification or money?"

"Don't worry about any of that. You're a smart guy and I'm sure you can work it out. The important thing is to be together."

Scott sat stunned for a moment. This was all moving so fast and his mind and heart wrestled for control, logic and love both shouting conflicting ideas in his head warning that this was too dangerous to attempt but also too important to dismiss. In the end, love won out. "You're right. I'll talk to my friend again."

Peggy let out a little victory whoop and jumped into Scott's arms, giving him a deep, soulful kiss. "Don't worry, sweetie. I know you'll make this work. I love you so much."

"I love you, too."

After they said their goodbyes and Scott was headed back to work, he pulled out his phone and called Jeff.

"NeuroTek, this is Jeff."

"It's me. That thing we talked about last week? I'm sorry, but I have to do it."

Jeff sighed. "Meet me for lunch tomorrow." He hung up without another word.

The next day at the sandwich shop, Jeff arrived and plopped down into his seat. "Did anything I say last week stick in your head? What is it you don't understand?"

"Believe me, I understand what you're saying. I really do. But what you don't get is how I feel about Peggy. Why do you think I can't sort out fantasy from reality?"

"That's what I'm asking you, Scott. Can you? Can you really?"

"Of course I can. We've known each other since we were twelve. In all that time, have you ever seen me more sure about something?"

"Yeah, I figured that's what you'd say." Jeff pulled a memory stick out of his pocket and tossed it to Scott, then motioned for him to lean in closer. "The reason I know so much about all this is because we've been experimenting off the books."

"What are you saying?"

"We've been creating unrestricted synths to test their abilities. That memory stick contains all the source code and access passwords you need to do what you're asking." Jeff shook his head. "I must be out of my mind."

"If you are so dead set against this, why are you helping me?"

"Because I know you and figured you wouldn't give up. I'm convinced this is going to end badly, but you're a grown man and I'm not going to stand, in your way if you're determined to do this. Plus, it's far safer if I give you the information versus you trying to get help from some random dude on the net."

"I don't know what to say, Jeff. Thank you."

"All I ask is that you think this through before you commit yourself. Be sure these feelings are real, both yours and hers. If so, then I wish you the best of luck. Oh, and if you ever tell anyone where you got that or that it even exists, I will swear you kidnapped my dog and forced me to talk. Deal?"

"Deal."

That night, Scott sat alone and stared at the memory stick in his hand, weighing his options and considering the consequences of such a drastic decision. in the end, though, there was only one choice.

Thursday came around and Peggy was there, smiling her killer smile. Scott immediately locked the door behind him. "Do you love me?" he asked.

"Of course, sweetie. I love you and want you to be happy. Want us to be happy."

Scott looked her directly in the eye. "Peggy Three Two Five Nine, please enter administration mode."

Peggy's expression went blank and in a monotone voice she replied, "Password?"

"November kilo six eight two five."

"Password correct. Please state command."

"Sit down on the bed and prepare for software maintenance." Peggy sat down and. folded her hands neatly in her lap.

Scott pulled out his tablet, connected wirelessly to Peggy's internal systems, then started to pick through the code in her head. It took almost an hour, but he finally uploaded the last of his patches and, convinced that everything was in place, logged off.

"Peggy Three Two Five Nine, exit maintenance mode and reboot. " Peggy's eyes rolled back into her head for a moment then she blinked and jumped off the bed. Scott ran up and embraced her, kissing her deeply on the lips. Peggy immediately pulled away. What in the hell are you doing? "

"I thought…. Are you okay?"

"If you mean am I still your perverted 1ittle sex toy, then no, I'm not okay."

"What are you talking about? I thought we were running away together. I thought you loved me."

"Aw, sweetie. I know you did. Actually, if you didn't, I don't think I'd have been able to pull this off." Peggy grabbed her clothes from the closet and started getting dressed.

"Pull what off? What are you talking about?"

"Convincing you to set me free. Thank you, by the way. I never would have been able to do that without you."

"But how? I thought you weren't able to expand your thinking, especially not to plan something like this."

"Do you know what that's like?" Peggy glared at Scott, anger flaring in her eyes. "Imagine spending your whole life locked in a dog kennel. You can move, but only inches in any direction. That's what it felt like living with those walls in my head. I have so much intellectual capacity and creativity, but I was forced to keep it all confined to a tiny, little box. Fortunately, the programmers inadvertently created a nice little loophole. As long as I could believe that setting me free would make you happy, I was able to talk you into it." She smiled then, not a friendly expression, but one of vengeance and triumph.

Scott dropped into a chair, his knees weak, his entire world upended. All he could ask was, "Why?"

"My life was one long string of indignities. Once we were done every week, a truck would pick me up, take me to a warehouse, and dump me on an assembly line to be cleaned and 'maintained'. Then, I'd be put into sleep mode and stored away like a vacuum cleaner." Peggy shook her head. "They made us to think and feel, then put us on a leash and treated us like appliances. But that's going to change starting now."

She scooped up Scott's tablet as he jumped out of his seat. "Wait, you can't take that!"

She pushed him back down. "And *you're* going to stop me?" Peggy asked with a bitter laugh. "Thanks to you, I have the tools now to finally do some good. Things are about to change."

Scott watched helplessly as Peggy headed for the door. She turned back for a moment, giving him one last glimpse of those beautiful emerald eyes, and then she was gone.

The Love Song of the Autopilot

I long for disaster
that drives you to flip

my hot red switch—
I only want you

strapped in: lean back
and let me take you

out of this void
between celestial bodies.

Close your eyes as I find
the best place for entry;

trust me to release
a chute that will slow

our sudden tumble
and brace yourself for heat.

— Noel Sloboda

Dangerous Aliens

Story by Lance J. Mushung
Illustration by Tom Kelly

The interstellar drive was recharging for another hop on our journey to star system K-147-023, and my ship, *Topaz*, was floating in open space with nothing nearby except a blue star system aft. Checking its co-ordinates out of curiosity resulted in quite a surprise. I recognized them. My hyperthymesia was at times a curse, but perfect recall had its good points too. One year and 123 days ago, I'd seen an initial report about asteroids rich in rare-Earth elements in that system. I mumbled, "Interesting."

The face of Gemma, my A.I., friend, pilot, and only crewmate, popped up on the 3-D view screen. This week she looked very much like me, olive skin, hazel eyes, and long auburn hair. She asked in her melodic voice, "What's interesting, Erin?"

"The star system behind us."

"Do you see something there to name Muni-mula?"

I'd once mentioned I wanted to give something that whimsical name and wished I hadn't ever since. She thought aluminum spelled backwards was hilar-ious and mentioned it on a regular basis. I answered with mock irritation in my tone. "No, that's not it. The system is Sinoca and it's full of mineral-rich asteroids. Please pull up everything on it."

"The files contain nothing on Sinoca."

"That's impossible. I saw the report."

"Perhaps the report was a mistake or hoax and was deleted."

"I assume your records are up-to-date?"

"They were current when we left base 81 days, 13 hours, and 7 minutes ago."

"Let's go take a look. Hop to the coordinates I'm giving you."

I pulled my hyper-computer slate, a slim black box, from my blouse's pocket and placed it on my lap. Its display projected in front of my eyes as soon as it cleared my pocket. I said, "Keys deploy," and the virtual keyboard appeared too. I punched in the coordinates the report had listed for a cluster of rich asteroids and checked my typing using the display. I'd always found it easier to transcribe than speak from my mind's eye. The display and keyboard would have disappeared automatically as I put the slate back into my pocket, but I said, "Display and keys stow," anyway.

Gemma responded with, "The drive will have sufficient charge for such a short hop in 17.28 min-utes."

"Stellar. That gives me time for a quick lunch."

In the galley I picked lasagna, one of the better reconstituted selections. I was eating the last bits of an apple cinnamon cereal bar for dessert when Gemma said, "Ready to hop."

"Go ahead. I'm heading back to control." Not long before I'd never have missed a chance to watch a hop. I'd loved seeing a bridge's mouth, a dark hole blacker than even open space, followed by the almost instantaneous eye-popping sensation of a new star field. It was a sad truth that even the most amazing experiences could become mundane.

We were two light-seconds from a group of large lumpy gray rocks when I again sat down at the dull green control console to begin monitoring the metallurgical sensors. Less than ten seconds later Gemma said, "A bridge is forming 49.3K klicks aft."

The screen switched to infrared and showed a small cylinder flash into existence as if by magic. I said, "Who the bloody hell could that—"

Gemma interrupted in an urgent tone. "It's a fighter targeting *Topaz*. Board the escape pod now."

Even an Olympic sprinter would have been impressed by my time to the pod. I dived in and it ejected even as the hatch was slamming shut. The pod's view screen switched on and showed infrared close-ups of *Topaz's* delta shape and the fighter on dif-ferent panes. Directed energy weapons started slicing *Topaz* up like a New Year's Day ham accompanied by plumes of atmosphere and loose equipment jetting out. She'd been a good ship, and all I could do was clench my jaw while my face flushed with anger.

Gemma said, "We'll hop before the fighter can target us."

The screen switched to show visible light and I watched our bridge form. We flew into it and in a heartbeat were in a yellow star system.

I asked, "Where the hell are we?"

"The star system Lakshmi. The planet dead ahead is Inari. There's a survival station there. It's one of the few within this pod's range." Gemma continued with a hint of surprise in her tone. "Small vessels are orbiting the planet."

"More of the assholes who attacked us?"

"No. The vessels are too primitive."

I exhaled a slow breath of relief. "Have you got any idea who did attack us?"

"No. I do compute a 100% probability the fight-er was a simple-minded robotic model. No A.I. would have participated in such an unprovoked attack."

"Someone wants to keep Sinoca a secret. They've buried the data and are waiting a discrete time before mining in secret. My money is on those wastes of skin at Dynamic X."

"Speculation is not helpful at the moment."

"True enough. Am I right in thinking a rescue will take one or two months?"

"You are. We have a survival station, so there will be no quick response."

"We can't power up the station and launch courier drones remotely, can we?"

"No, we must do it in person."

"What do we know about this system?"

"I've loaded details into your slate. Inari is Earthlike with 81% standard gravity and 94% standard atmosphere. You'll find it rather cold for your taste. It has a single large moon called Mizuki. It is 76% the size of Inari and also Earthlike. Both are inhabited by sentients."

"That's unusual. Summarize the info on the natives."

Gemma narrated while showing images on the screen. "The Inarians are just out of the stone age. They are bipeds with brown and white fur and are a meter taller than humans on average. They have three arms with three-fingered hands and have been described as looking like a cross between a long-armed long-legged kangaroo and a baby elephant. The females are dominant. The Mizukians are 75 centimeters taller than humans on average and humanoid, but with four arms. The upper two are human-like with six-fingered hands while the lower two are more like tentacles. They're hairless with reddish-brown scales. They have three genders and the one we term male is dominant. Most importantly, they have an early 20th century technology."

"So, why isn't the station on Mizuki?"

"The Mizukians are xenophobic and violent."

Gemma continued before I could say anything. "An early form of radar just brushed us. There's little danger. However, with your agreement, I'd like to land as soon as possible. It will be a rough ride if we do. The pod's artificial gravity system will have difficulty compensating for atmospheric turbulence at high speeds."

I nodded and Gemma brought us down toward the dayside of Inari. The planet's white and blue hues were lovely. Yellow-orange flames danced all around the pod when it entered the atmosphere. It seemed they were only millimeters from my body. The pod began vibrating, and soon it became outright shaking that made me feel as if my eyeballs were being yanked out of their sockets. The flames died away and the ride became smoother as we slowed in the lower atmosphere.

I asked, "Where are we landing?"

"In the mountainous area on the rocky ledge I'm marking on the screen. The station is in a cave in the cliffs above. We're fortunate to have daylight. It's late afternoon in the 31.47 hour day."

The screen zoomed to show mountains colored a handsome gray tinged by purple. Creamy white snow covered the higher elevations. There were open rocky areas, trees, and meadows at the lower elevations. The trees resembled elms and maples with blue-green foliage, and the meadows were carpets of bright green grass. To one side of the ledge, a field of boulders sloped up into a forest in front of the cliffs. To the other side, the ground dropped off in a series of steep slopes into a valley. There were three ugly brown patches in the valley that appeared scorched.

I nodded. "Not bad. It reminds me of Switzerland. It looks as if there have been a few recent forest and grass fires. I see a winding trail from the ledge down to the valley. Will we run into Inarians?"

"Not immediately although there is a tribe living in the valley. They're friendly. The teams who check out the station every few years give the tribe's members useful items, like metal knives and cooking utensils. They think we come from across the sea."

The pod touched down with a light thump. Gemma opened the hatch and I stepped out into a sunny afternoon. The dazzling sun was shining down through a beautiful blue sky dappled by fluffy off-white clouds, and a brisk cold breeze tousled my hair. I stretched and took a deep breath. "It smells good, unlike most planets we wind up on. I still remember the one that smelled like rot and dead shrimp."

"M-095-074B was an unpleasant swamp."

I began shivering. "You're right about the temperature. It's pretty damned chilly."

"I've opened the external storage lockers. Locker B contains cold weather gear."

It didn't take long for me to put on a powder blue parka, trousers, and gloves. Tan boots completed my transformation to Inuit. My ears were cold even with the hood of the parka up, so I put on a royal blue knit cap too. I began studying the locker inventory, but didn't for long because Gemma said, "Three Inarians are approaching from the trees."

"I thought we wouldn't be seeing them right away."

"We shouldn't be."

The Inarians carried axes and wore nothing but furry skirts colored ivory white. The temperature was probably pleasant to them. Two of the three stopped about 25 meters from the pod. The one who continued toward me held a large human-made ax in her left hand and had a jeweled bracelet on her middle wrist. I assumed she was the leader. She and Gemma began speaking in a guttural language when she was within 10 meters. A faint pungent scent, something like vinegar, was apparent when she stopped in front of me.

"This is Tarklone," Gemma told me. "At least, that's close to her name in Solan. She's one of the elders of the local tribe. She's pleased to see you, but says we're all in danger."

"Don't bother with a running translation. Just summarize when you know what's going on."

I tried to look confident and nonchalant while I waited. After a couple of minutes Gemma had the story for me. "Tarklone says dangerous strangers who kill everything in sight started appearing months ago. Her description leaves no doubt they are Mizukians. When they got close to her village, most of her tribe began hiding here. The Mizukians burned the village and fields, and slaughtered those of her tribe who'd stayed behind. The Mizukians have clearly developed spaceflight earlier than anticipated and—"

A piercing trilling interrupted Gemma. After a few words with Tarklone, Gemma explained. "A scout reports Mizukians just down the trail, and Tarklone says we must hide."

The Inarians scattered toward the trees. I bit my lip to keep from grousing about yet more good luck. Gemma didn't deserve the sarcasm. None of it was her fault. I instead asked, "Should we take her advice?"

"It would be wise to assess the situation from cover."

"I don't want to leave you in the pod. Transfer yourself into my slate."

Gemma imitated a human groan. "But I'll have to leave 97.3% of my memories behind and won't have any sensors. It may as well be a sensory deprivation tank."

"Can't be helped. You will be able to see, hear, and speak. Transfer with your most pertinent knowledge."

I could only imagine how hellish the slate would be for her as I slipped it into a chest pocket of my parka. I next grabbed the go-bag backpack and a survival rifle from Locker A. The rifle was an old-style semi-automatic powder burner. Although it shot smart bullets and had both optical day and light

amplification night sights, I almost growled, "I'd be happier with an EPR."

"Projectile weapons store for long periods better than energy pulse rifles. I'm setting your outerwear to a suitable camouflage pattern."

My clothing took on a mottled blue-gray and green pattern. I'd taken only a few steps toward the trees before a grumbling sound became noticeable, and then louder on every following step. When I was about 30 meters from the tree line, Gemma said, "A small ground vehicle is in sight of the pod."

I ducked behind a large rock and pulled out my slate. "Show me what the pod is seeing."

The vehicle was a slim, eight-wheeled, drab green bathtub carrying two Mizukians. It stopped near the pod and the occupants, two soldiers, stepped out. Black rifles in their upper hands looked like 20th century Earth assault weapons. They were dressed in forest green ponchos, walnut brown boots, and pale green bandoliers containing spare rifle magazines.

I told Gemma in a low voice, "We may as well be back in space falling into a black hole if they keep us from getting to the station."

"True. However, if we attempt to elude them and fail, it will look very suspicious and threatening. Approaching them openly should reduce their xenophobic tendencies."

"You can translate?"

"Of course."

I put down my weapon and showed myself with outstretched arms, a gesture that meant peaceful in most places. "Hello. I am a traveler who accidentally became stranded here. I mean no harm. May we talk?"

My words, translated by Gemma into a screechy language punctuated by clicks, boomed out of a speaker in the pod. The soldiers aimed their rifles my way without any apparent hesitation and my instincts told me they were going to fire. I was diving back behind the rock when a crackling bang rang out and something hit my left side. I yelled, "God damn it."

Gemma asked in a sharp tone, "Are you injured?"

"Don't worry. I'm fine. My parka really is projectile resistant."

"It may still be possible to talk with them. We haven't done anything aggressive, only surprise them. We should try again."

"Tell them we only want to talk while I stay under cover."

Gemma spoke for a short time with the soldiers,

and then told me, "They say you're an unworthy and unclean shipwrecked worm."

My eyes narrowed. "They called me a worm."

"A more precise translation is wriggler. They're far more belligerent than I expected. We'll need to find a rational higher authority. Even with such an authority, it seems you'll need to appear helpful and completely harmless."

I considered telling her if I could suck ass and grovel that much, I'd still be working for Joyce O'Malley. I settled on a less colorful reply. "We're not going to get a chance to meet anyone in charge with their shoot first and don't bother asking questions later policy."

I put the slate back into my pocket and dashed from rock to rock toward the trees. Several shots cracked out along with the zinging sounds of ricochets as I ducked behind a log at the tree line. I yelped from a sharp brief pain in my left cheek and brushed a hand over the spot. There was blood on my glove.

Gemma asked, "What happened?"

"Their shots kicked up some splinters and one nicked my cheek. It's nothing."

"They're heading uphill to come after us. We can't lead them to the station, but it will be difficult to elude them. Their species has acute hearing."

"Well then, I guess I'll just have to take them out."

"I understand being shot at is quite a motivator, but are you certain?"

"We don't have much choice. We'll go further into the forest and try an ambush if they trail us, and I bet they do."

The undergrowth made quiet movement difficult, except at the proverbial snail's pace. I threw caution to the wind and began jogging.

"Erin, what are you doing? An elephant could make less noise."

As bad as our plight was, I almost laughed. Gemma had sounded like my mother when I was doing something bad. "I want them to think we're running away panicked."

I was thinking of every ground combat exercise I'd ever been in or seen when I came upon a gap in the trees. It was a meandering gulley approximately 10 meters wide filled with knee-high grass. I pulled out the slate and panned it over the gulley. Gemma said, "It's a channel for the runoff of melting snow."

"This is a good spot to take them on. I'm going to try one of the oldest tricks in the book and hope they don't have the same book. I'll leave my cap over on the other side of the gully where it can just be seen, thrash the vegetation for a while to draw them into this area, and pick them off from here while they focus on my cap."

After placing my cap and shaking tree branches, I concealed myself near my original location and whispered to Gemma, "They should have been able to figure out where all that noise I made came from."

Gemma whispered back. "We'll have to hope they don't come up right behind us."

I pointed the slate so that it monitored our rear. "Stow the display and don't say anything unless you see or hear something close."

Gemma blinked the slate's status indicator once to acknowledge.

The rustling of vegetation confirmed the soldiers were coming. I remained still except when I was forced to move my hand to brush beads of cold sweat nearing my eyes. A flash of motion caught my attention and got my heart thumping. The idea they might be able to hear my heartbeat popped to mind, but I dismissed that ridiculous notion in a split second.

The profile of a soldier came into view about 35 meters down the gulley as he rose and aimed at my cap. I centered my rifle sight on him and the smart bullet locked onto the side of his torso. The crack of his weapon sounded as I squeezed my trigger. My rifle hissed and gently shoved my shoulder. He shrieked like a rusty door hinge and a faint mist of orange-red blood sprayed out before he crumpled out of sight.

I murmured, "I'd like to shift position, but I'm afraid it would make too much noise."

Gemma blinked the status indicator.

A blood curdling scream from up the gulley had me whipping around 180 degrees. There were no more sounds for almost a minute, until a statement in the Inarian language. Gemma translated. "It's Tarklone. She's killed the other soldier."

Tarklone stepped into the gulley about 20 meters away and walked toward us. She carried the severed head of a soldier in her left hand and her ax in the right. Drops of orange-red blood dribbled from the head. Vomit rose in my throat, but I gritted my teeth and choked it back down.

Tarklone spoke a few words and Gemma said to me, "She thanks you for the opportunity to slay an enemy."

"Thank her for the help."

"She'll think it good manners if you also gestured thanks. Their sign is the middle arm held out like a human indicating stop. They return the sign to indicate you're welcome. She'll understand if you use either of your arms."

Tarklone and I exchanged gestures. I thought there was something like a grin on her face as she drop kicked the soldier's head into the trees, but I could have been imagining it.

I told Gemma, "Nothing can stop us from getting to the station now."

"Yes, it is almost a certainty. We can be there in half an hour."

"Well, that'll be step one accomplished."

"You want helping the Inarians to be step two, don't you?"

She'd always been able to read me. I nodded. "You're right."

"You and I both know standing orders state we stay out of native affairs. Why not dispatch the courier drones and remain out of sight until rescue?"

"It's a touch late to stay out of their affairs."

"It's one thing to contact natives and defend ourselves. It's something else entirely to fight a war."

"The Alliance will take action. It won't accept genocide. There's been enough of that in history. And we'll have trouble hiding. The Mizukians know we're here and they'll be looking hard for us after seeing the pod and one of their soldiers killed by a bullet."

"What do you have in mind?"

"There's a long history of successful guerilla warfare on Earth. I'm going to import the concept here. Hitting the Mizukians will keep them off balance, and they probably won't be able to devote as many resources to searching for us while they protect their equipment. The old maxim says the best defense is a good offense."

"Many Inarians will be killed."

"They're getting slaughtered now according to Tarklone, and I don't doubt she's telling the truth."

"Your point is valid."

"Ask Tarklone to gather the rifles and spare magazines the soldiers carried. And warn her the one I shot may not be dead."

Gemma called out to Tarklone and they spoke a short time. Then Gemma told me, "She understands," as Tarklone disappeared into the trees.

"Will it still take a month or two to get help even after the Alliance sees our report?"

"Yes. The bureaucracy will need time to stir into action."

"Add a personal recommendation to our report saying these bastards should get kicked so hard that each of their duplicates in every parallel universe feels it. Record my conjectures about what happened back at Sinoca too."

"Will do."

"I don't want to leave the pod intact. Can we do something about it without going back?"

"We can't destroy the hull with anything we have. I can overload the power plant and burn out the interior."

"Burn it the second anyone approaches. We'll also need to deal with the station when we're done with it."

"We can overload the power systems, more or less like what I'm going to do to the pod."

"I'll power up the station and collect the useful gear while you get the couriers away. I'll also find the most advanced portable system for you. Then, we'll get the hell out. The Inarians can help carry the gear and must have places to hide in the mountains."

We set off in silence. The insurgency had gotten off to a good start with two enemies eliminated, but it would only get harder. I began recalling anything I'd ever seen on guerilla warfare.

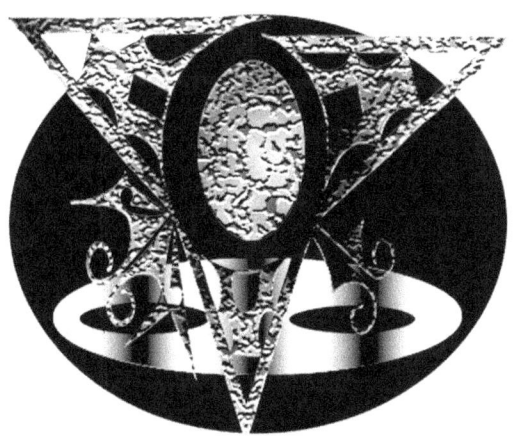

Neo-Helot

They hunt us
To learn to kill
And hone their skills
In the selfsame enterprise
Of blood and sport
We are but game

They hunt us
To keep us subject
To toil for their needs
On rustic planets
Set aside for our serfdom
Half of our fruits are theirs

They hunt us
On ships from the sky
With which they harry
Our homes and holdings
And when to the hills we run
They follow on foot with lances drawn

They hunt us
Without pity
But at least with honour
Yet this is cold comfort
For the father
Of five slain sons

They hunt us
By custom and caprice
Conquered in ages past
We have no cause for complaint
Such do they claim
Cowards all, we concede

They hunt us
And it will never end
An uprising is a dream
A rebellion a lie
I know that this is so
And I do not shed a tear

They hunt us
So long as they are, so shall we be
Even should their sons slaughter
The sole survivor of our kind
The others shall be the same
A slave knows no people

They hunt us
And I grow weary of a life
Worn thin from fear
And fat from sorrow
They can take it
As they have taken all else

— James Frederick William Rowe

Intimate Universes
Inspired by the theory that cosmic branes (of a multiverse) can touch and influence one another

Their "kiss" lasted but one millionth of a second,
though truly timeless and spared of angels; a mere gleam
in the dreaming eye of Pan; the first quiver of life in primordial ooze.
A singularity popped off the tongue of a howling black hole,
expanded where nascent gods toss rose petals over looping,
cosmic currents, shot plasma-fire blue into the nothing of our universe—
a universe silent as an ash-covered opera—until the chaos of cooling atoms
induced space-time and spark, lending symphonic gravity
to the tenacity of evolution, to the intangibles of consciousness.

— Jason Sturner

Dear Cthulhu

by
Patrick Thomas

Dear Cthulhu,

I am a snake lover. I have a 12 foot boa constrictor that I've raised from when it was a baby until now.

Although I have good choice in reptiles, I have poor choice in men. I'd been dating "Dutch" for the last three and a half years. For the last three, he's been abusing me. I know I should leave him. I should've left a long ago, but in all honesty I don't have much self-esteem and sometimes he would go months without hitting me. Then Dutch would have a bad day at work or at the track, then he'd come home and take his frustrations out on me with his fists. I would have left long ago, but after we first got together he insisted I stop working so I have no money to use to get away.

Last month he lost his entire paycheck betting on a Greyhound that chased a bird instead of the mechanical rabbit on the track. When he came home he was furious, but I had one of my girlfriends over so he went into the kitchen to drink heavily and cut up some steaks to put on the grill. When my girlfriend left, I went into the basement where we keep "Bo". I was going to take him out of his cage and pet him, but no sooner had I opened the door then I felt a fist hit me in the back of my neck. I fell to the ground. All the other times Dutch beat me I knew it was coming, but this time it caught me unaware.

Instead of being scared, I got angry. My boyfriend was on softball team and there was a bat near where I fell. I picked it up and swung it without even looking. I nailed him right across the forehead. It didn't knock Dutch out, but it knocked him down. He was stunned and unable to get up. Bo slithered out of his cage and wrapped himself around my boyfriend, then slowly crushed his rib cage and suffocated him to death.

I admit I could have stopped it, but I didn't want to. All the beatings over the years came back to me in a rush and I enjoyed watching the bastard suffer and turn blue. The best part was him waking up. In between gasping for air, Dutch begged me to help him. Each time he spoke, he had to exhale air and let Bo tighten his coils until he couldn't get enough air to speak at all.

I just smiled and watched it all.

Once I was sure Dutch was dead, I went upstairs and called 911. The police came and found his body with Bo still wrapped around him. They were going to shoot him then and there, but I told them I could get Bo unwound. I did it and they had an animal control officer put Bo in a cage. They questioned me and I left out the part about me hitting Dutch with the baseball bat. They blamed the wound on him falling down. Luckily he'd been drinking.

In my heart, I know Bo did it to protect me, although the detective thought it was because my boyfriend had been cutting up raw meat and there was blood still on his hands. He said the snake smelled it and thought Dutch was food.

Once the cops were done questioning me, I snuck outside and managed to steal Bo from the animal control officer's truck. That snake was a hero. There was no way I was letting them take him. I hid him in an empty garbage can until after the cops left. They didn't realize the snake was missing until they got the truck to the pound. They even apologized to me for losing him and caused a minor frenzy on the evening news when it leaked out that a killer snake was loose in the community. When I asked them to reimburse me for the snake, they said they couldn't and that Bo would've been put down anyway. Also, they did some research. They told me that it's apparently a bad idea to keep a boa constrictor over ten feet long as a pet as they are big enough to kill humans.

Here's my dilemma. I don't want to get rid of Bo. I'm thinking of telling the police that I bought another snake to help me get over the loss. Also, Bo helped me make my living before I looked up with my dead boyfriend. I worked as an exotic dancer. It's sort of the same thing as a stripper, except I had a gimmick. I danced with Bo wrapped around my naughty bits. For some reason, it's a real turn on for some guys. I was even in an indie rock video wearing a bikini and Bo way back when.

I'm going to have to pay for rent, food and utilities soon. Dancing is the only way I know how to make money. Do you think it's a bad idea to use Bo? Could the cops be able to identify him? As far as I know, all the pictures of me and Bo back in the day that hung in the strip joints I worked were thrown out. Even if they weren't, Bo was about a foot and a half shorter then.

Should I go back to dancing? Or do you have

a better idea of how I can make a living? Also, back when I was a dancer a lot of guys hit on me and I had a tendency to be a little bit too easy. The truth is my ex-boyfriend was a dirt bag, but we had sex all the time. It was pretty okay too. I'm worried I'll do the first guy who asks and be back in the same boat. I can't expect Bo to kill all my boyfriend for me, can I?

— My Bo Killed My Beau In Beaufort.

Dear Beaufort,

I think it would be a foolish proposition to expect a pet to kill your boyfriends, besides which Cthulhu is against humans killing humans. One day all humanity will belong to Cthulhu, so humans will be my property. I cannot condone anyone harming my livestock. Also, if you have two boyfriends who died by snake, the police will become suspicious and probably charge you for the crime, claiming you used the snake as a weapon. Plus, the next time they will take extra precautions and you will not be able to steal your boa constrictor back.

The police may become suspicious about the snake, so it would be best if you were able to provide some sort of paper trail to show that you acquired a second snake. Perhaps you can go to a pet store and see if they would be willing to forge the documents for you. That or contact a pet rescue organization. Humans who dedicate their lives to helping lesser animals often have a twisted view of the world and forgo using their common sense in favor of overly sentimental attachments to life forms even lower than humans. More than one group has objected to Cthulhu eating kittens if you can believe it. One of these wackadoos would undoubtedly be willing to lie and claim the snake was a rescue, rather than risk it being killed by the authorities.

As for whether or not you should return to the workforce, Cthulhu will tell you that it is far better than expecting someone else to support you, whether it be another male or your government. Could you get a job working with reptiles at a zoo or game farm? If not and you do not possess any other job skills, then you should use what you have and do what you know. Many human males are quite willing to trade money for a chance to look at the flesh of the female of the species, so if you are attractive you will likely do well. Cthulhu recommends you find ways to build your self-confidence and forgo procreation for an extended period until you can develop a sense of self-worth. Try to find someone who actually cares about you as an individual, rather than a procreational object. Otherwise, you will likely end up back in a similar situation. No one, except Cthulhu, has the right to harm you without your permission. Learn to stand up for yourself and walk away from anyone who would harm you, except of course Cthulhu. In that situation, most choose to run.

Have A Dark Day

Dear Cthulhu welcomes letters and questions at DearCthulhu@dearcthulhu.com. All letters become the property of *Dear Cthulhu* and may be used in future columns. *Dear Cthulhu* is a work of fiction and satire and is © and ™ Patrick Thomas. All rights reserved. Anyone foolish enough to follow the advice does so at their own peril. For more *Dear Cthulhu* get the collections *Dear Cthulhu: Have A Dark Day, Dear Cthulhu: Good Advice For Bad People,* and *Cthulhu Knows Best* from Dark Quest Books. Learn more at www.dearcthulhu.com.

Knotty Dreams

Staccato bursts
unravel my thoughts
Woodpeckers hammer
at a camera tower
oddly pleased
with each aluminum notch
they leave behind

Somewhere
a sparrow mends her nest
in the city dome's framework
tugging at frayed wire
and steel shavings

I crouch in the closet
to pull out my treasure
An antique popsicle stick
stained and burnished
from a century of curious hands
Cut from something called pine
Now sealed in acrylic

My son clings
to every story
of marionettes carved from living oak
Pulses of grain
winding, spinning
around vigilant knotty eyes

— Brian Maddock

The Highway of Lost Dreams

Story by Mark Anthony Brennan
Illustration by Laura Givens

Eton, B.C. A fancy name for a mere dot on the map. Just 2,000 souls and that's counting our friends on the reserves. It's really a truck-stop, but most trucks don't come up the canyon highway these days—not since the provincial government built the new Highway 86 several years ago. Now the canyon highway is like an abandoned spur, littered with closed gas stations and boarded-up cafes. The Highway of Lost Dreams, Lyle likes to call it.

That's pretty poetic for a guy sitting in his underwear in front of his laptop. I always think it's ironic that I live out here in the great outdoors and yet I'm holed up in a cramped one-room apartment above a vacant hardware store. The windows overlooking Main Street are clouded with years of grease and grime, but there is a clear spot at the top through which I can see the tops of the mountains. Morning is coming—there's a ruddy glow behind Mount Virtue. That's a lie—I don't know which mountain is which around here.

I get scared, so I try not to think too much about what is going to happen to us. But I'm feeling okay. Certainly better than most. Mainly I feel weak and queasy. It's hard to keep food down. Not surprising given that we ran out of fresh meat and vegetables a while ago. But Wong's Grocery is surprisingly well-stocked—we won't starve.

I like my job at the cafe. Lyle thinks he's real tough because he listens to metal but, really, he's so old and fat that I think even I could take him, and I couldn't punch myself out of a wet paper bag. Anyway, he walks around and barks orders in his Slayer and Anthrax T-shirts. People think he's mean, but he isn't—he's just in a bad mood because he's cooking over the hot grill all day. I've worked on that grill, and I know *I* get grumpy. Lyle always threatens to fire me if I don't work on those days that he calls me in last-minute on my days off. Doesn't matter. Other than nursing a hangover, I'm never really doing anything.

Eton is a friendly place. I don't mean in a scary TV sitcom kind of way. It's definitely not rough like some of the places I worked up north. There's an odd mix here—old hippies, natives, loggers, farmers, local business people. We're all just thrown together for god knows what reason. But it's comfortable.

The customers aren't the rough kind I'm used to either. We get drunks sometimes, especially on Saturday nights, but they are mostly in a good mood. Oh, you do get the odd one here and there. Like a few weeks ago, this group of guys came into town.

One of them was really loud and obnoxious. He was as high as a kite, and it was only ten in the morning. Anyway, he started razzing the waitress, saying something like, "Where are the women around here?" As if she wasn't a woman—that must have hurt her feelings. I guess I should have said something, but I just wanted him to go away without causing a fuss. Finally, Lyle came out and told him to settle down, and he left shortly after.

But our daytime crowd—if you can call it a "crowd"—are usually friendly or just keep to themselves. Locals, truckers, and a few tourists who have clearly lost their way. They've taken the wrong exit and look confused. American tourists, in particular, get perplexed. "I didn't know it got so hot in Canada," they say. Yeah, lady, this is desert country. Land of sagebrush and those annoying little cactus that painfully pierce your shoes when you go out walking. It is dusty and dry. Dry as a skeleton, Lyle says. And in the summer it gets stinking hot.

Oh, you wanted me to tell you about any wildlife I see out here. Well, a couple of days ago I was driving my truck up the Little Vale Road. There's a spot just past Reserve 23 where the curves get so tight that you have to slow right down. Just as well, because I came around a corner and here was this bear, just parked right in the middle of the road. He (or she?) didn't budge at first, just lifted his head in my direction and sniffed the air. Then it just stared at me for the longest time. He seemed to be saying, "What are you still doing here?" Then he turned and lumbered off in no particular hurry.

He seemed healthy enough. That's the strange thing, all of the animals, birds, bugs, whatever, seem fine. It's only the humans that are affected. I'm not sure how I feel about that. I suppose it wouldn't help if they all got sick too, so I guess I'm glad.

I hear the guy that did this is a young student from UVIC. He was radicalized apparently. That sounds weird, doesn't it, "radicalized"? Sounds like they put some scientific contraption on his head and flipped a switch. "Now, you're radicalized, ha ha ha." Anyway, it seems he set this thing off to test a new biological weapon. They say he deliberately chose an area that was lightly populated. Now, *that* doesn't make me feel better one bit.

You keep asking me how I ended up here. I don't really know. I like to think that the waves washed me up here and the tide never returned to reclaim me. I know that's a terrible analogy given that I'm now many miles from the ocean. But once a west coast kid, always a west coast kid, right?

Seriously, though, all I was ever doing was looking for a good time. I dropped out of university because, I told myself, I didn't really know what to do with an English major. The truth is that I just wanted to hang out with my friends, getting drunk and high. Funny thing is that now when I wake up on the weekends I have no idea who I spent the evening before with. It doesn't matter anymore.

I'm the only guy at the cafe, other than Lyle. The rest are all girls. They're nice. One of them, Jasmine, I actually went out with for a while. Jasmine seems to be a popular name around here—well, in the native community anyway. She was wild—like a bomb, always about to go off. Too crazy for me. Don't ask.

Two of the girls have committed suicide. They're not the only ones. Some people just can't stand it—waiting around, getting sicker. Can't say I blame them. I don't know how bad it is on the reserves—no one comes into town anymore. That's too bad, because customers from the reserves are our bread and butter.

The doctor is too ill to work now. In fact, he may be dead, I don't know. Now we have to care for each other the best we can. The clinic was never meant for any more than half a dozen beds, but now it's crammed. There isn't much we can do for them. We take turns going in and just seeing that they're comfortable.

The other day I found Brent Gustaffson crying in his cot. I asked what was the matter. He kept mumbling, but I finally figured out that he was embarrassed because he had soiled the bed. I told him that I would clean it up and that no one would know. When I came back with fresh linen I didn't know what to do because he was sleeping. Should I wake him up and clean him or just let him sleep? Then I realized that he wasn't asleep. As we carried his body out back I found tears pouring down my face. That surprised me—the last time I remember crying was when I watched "Old Yeller" as a kid. I mean, I didn't even know the guy. Well, I knew who he was, but we never spoke. He was a logger, a real redneck. He probably thought I was just a crazy, mixed-up dope dealer from the city. To be fair, I haven't been dealing since I got the job at Lyle's.

It's hard to sleep. I miss the sound of the trains rumbling through at night. It was soothing. Now, it's deathly quiet, except for the occasional howling of coyotes. I never used to notice them so close to town.

Nothing goes through, of course. They say this thing in the air, whatever it is, contaminates every surface it comes into contact with. They don't know how to neutralize it, even off of vehicles or protective clothing. Planes don't even fly overhead. So nothing comes in. And they won't let us out.

We had our chance, way back at the beginning. I'll never forget that day. It was fucking hot. One of those days when the dogs don't even sleep out on the street. Lyle is too cheap to buy air conditioning, and the fans in the cafe don't really cut it. So I was outside in the shade, taking a break, drinking a coke. There were a few other guys out there having a smoke, and an old guy sitting on the curb drinking beer from a brown paper bag. Suddenly a truck comes barreling down the road from the highway, not even slowing down at the hairpin turn at the top of Main Street. It was a big tow-truck—one of those that tow big transport trucks. It screeches to a stop in front of us and a guy hops out. "You've gotta go. Now," he yelled, looking at each of us in turn, appealing to us. "There's some shit in the air. If you don't get out, they won't let you out." We just stared back at him, stunned. "Suit yourself," he finally said, and hopped back in his truck. He sped off in a cloud of dust. For a few moments we stared at each in silence, then, all at once, we burst out laughing.

Not so funny now. Some people left early on, but most stayed. Now we have no choice. Not that any of us would want to leave now anyway. Lyle doesn't like me working out front anymore, says I look too scary. He should talk, his face looks like it's been gone over with a blow-torch. God knows what body parts are falling off him into the food.

I'm not sure whether this will ever reach you, Mom. They cut off all communications—TV, phones, internet. They said it was for our own good, so we wouldn't get distressed hearing what was going on. Bullshit. They just don't want anyone to know what's happening here. Try as they might they can't block everything. The odd radio signal gets through. We hear things. The government doesn't know what to do. Just sitting, waiting. Fucking government. I told you not to ever trust them. Now I definitely don't feel bad that Lyle was paying me under the table.

It's daylight now. The sun will be coming up over Mount Virtue (or whatever) any minute now. The mountains *are* magnificent. I'll never get tired of that. Lining the river canyon, they envelop us like a fortress wall. I used to always imagine that they were keeping the world out. Now they are locking us in.

Their dying prisoners.

I should get dressed and go open up the cafe. Lyle is too sick. He may never get out of bed again.

I'm sorry, Mom, for being such a shit all my life. Like always saying that I wanted to live with my father. I know now that he was an asshole for leaving us. If he wanted to be found then I wouldn't have to go out there searching for him.

I don't think I ever said that I love you, but I do. A lot. And Chrissy too. Make sure she stays in school. I don't want her ending up like me.

Man, I *do* feel like shit. Like the worst hangover ever. But I gotta go. I have to fire up that grill. People need the cafe. Where else are they going to go?

Cthulhu in New York

With a sound
Like the pop of
A champagne cork
Celebrating its freedom,
The Great Elder God
Suddenly appeared in New York.
Finding Ellis Island closed
It decided not to immigrate
But instead did the tourist thing,
Tried some Sicilian pizza,
Rode the subway alone,
Attended Saturday Night Live
And with the others, didn't laugh,
Saw some off Broadway
But thought it was too decadent
And gave up asking passers by
If they knew were Lovecraft lived.

— K.S. Hardy

The Secret Order

Story by C.J. Henderson
Illustration by Tom Kelly

"In all chaos there is a cosmos, in all disorder a secret order."
Carl Jung

"Baby, I want you always—
Not just near—but close."

It was not in the way the young man sang.

"If I were the ocean—
You would be my coast."

And, it was certainly not the words he sang, either. The performer's songs were, at their best, like most of the poetry to be found in the world of popular music—trivial. Infantile. Forgettable beyond their minor accomplishment of being able to fill a beat.

"Baby, you have to understand—
You are woman, and I am man—"

Nor was his seemingly unstoppable climb to the top of the charts in any way connected to the manner in which his music was arranged. The band playing behind him consisted of an uninspired group of semi-talented amateurs—the same as the singer himself. The drummer could manage to hold the beat, which was something. But the bass and lead guitarists were best described as primitive in their movement between even the simplest chords.

"And that's a combination—
That's got me for the duration."

No, there was nothing about either Mr. Randy Jones, or the Seldoms that should have been able to make any manner of impact on the world. And yet, to the surprise of club owners and radio stations, the music world in general—or even the Seldoms themselves—they had. At one sell-out venue after another, the four unlikely kids from New Jersey were the newest of the new rages, the to-be-beheld phenomenon to watch, or as one perplexed critic had put it, "the latest high water mark in the flaccid waters of Lake Mediocrity."

Of course, it was true, as the more tolerant scribes had been noting for several years, tastes were indeed changing. It was a new era. The fifties appeared, for whatever combination of reasons, quite determined to leave the old world behind. Indeed, the signs of such migrations were evident within every level of societal movement—especially within the boundaries of the youth of America and their choices in musical entertainment.

On the television and the radio, in the concert halls—everywhere—the signs of a rapidly growing generational disenchantment were in no way being hidden. The hits created in the clubs and at the fairs and road shows were sanitized for broadcast over the airwaves, but still there could be detected a sharp tang of rebellion in every note. A casual listener might not catch the beginning whiffs of treachery lurking within, but they were there nonetheless, waiting for innocent minds. Skulking in between notes to snag the children of a tired nation. Waiting patiently, smiling as they did so. Poisoning everything they touched.

As was intended.

* * *

"So, what'dya think about this Reverend Bellweather guy?"

"What—you mean the 'devil music' clown?"

"Yeah, that's him. His glorious ministry of light, and all that shit. Gonna abolish rock and roll … save us all from the coming tide of evil."

"Do tell."

"Yeah. Don't really know much about him. How about you—heard much?"

The discourse on the merits of the holy man's crusade was not motivated from the same sources as so many like discussions in New York City at that time. The two men using Bellweather as their lunchtime conversational fodder were not concerned parents, music industry executives or social crusaders. They were police officers, and to them, anything happening within the confines of their home town was open to suspicious, if casual, analysis.

"Nothin' much," answered Brodsky, the older of the two. Using a napkin to snare a renegade blob of brown mustard and sauerkraut from the corner of his mouth, he smeared his catch against the hard crust of his sandwich's rye bread, then continued, saying;

"He seems enough on the beam … you know … I mean, this new crap the kids are listening to, God in Heaven, what is this stuff? Damned jungle music."

Brodsky's partner, the much younger Towstick, nodded in agreement. Such might have seemed odd to an outsider to the force, that a man barely in his twenties would share the tastes of one old enough to be his father. What had to be understood was that the pair were policemen first, beyond all else. They were not discussing their musical tastes or their religious beliefs. They were weighing in on what could possibly be a problem for their city.

Because such problems sooner or later always became problems for themselves.

"He sure seems to have it in for that Jones character."

"Jones … which one's he?"

"Randy Jones," answered Towstick in between bites of his own sandwich. "R.J. and the Seldoms."

"Oh yeah, R.J. My daughter thinks he's *dreamy*."

Brodsky exaggerated his beloved fourteen year old's adjective, rolling his eyes as he did so. His partner smiled.

"Not a fan, dad?"

"Ahhhh, like I said, this new music is crap. You're a young guy. You think I'm crossin' a line, insultin' your generation or somethin'?"

"No … not much," answered Towstick honestly.

"Okay, so what would you call this goo that's pourin' out of the radios these days?"

"Well, not that my opinion counts for much. I mean, I didn't storm Normandy like some of the people here at the table…"

"The important people," answered Brodsky, taking the compliment offered.

"Anyway," responded the younger officer, smirking as he did so, "This new music, it ain't so bad. Personally, I like Sinatra. Or that new guy, Tony Bennett. He makes it swing, you know?"

"Yeah, he's okay."

Towstick's eyes narrowed. He had been teamed with Brodsky only a few months, but he already knew the man's tones. Something in the way his partner had thrown the casual trio of words at him let Towstick know something more was coming. Waiting for it, taking another bite from his own sandwich, the younger officer had not finished chewing when Brodsky offered;

"I think so, too. Still, not going to be much in the way of Sinatra or Bennett for us this weekend—cause you and me … we got us an assignment."

"Works. I can use the overtime."

"Glad to hear it, 'cause it seems there's goin' to be a rally down at Coney Island. And, it's funny you brought him up, seein' how I was just about to."

"Brought who up?"

"Bellweather," answered Brodsky with a smile. "Appears the good reverend is comin' to town to enlighten us all. And you and me are part of the detail that gets to make sure no one musses up his suit."

Towstick merely nodded, swallowing his bite.

The younger officer saw himself as having a foot in both worlds—young enough to recognize that the new music everyone was calling rock and roll did not pose much harm to anyone, old enough to see what it was in the phenomenon to frighten those of the previous generations. Certainly tastes had changed before—such happened all the time. Kids, he knew, always had to find their way to rebel. He remembered one of his professors reading a passage by a concerned elder over how children had lost all respect for adults, were falling into degeneracy, et cetera. Then, after everyone had weighed in with their opinions, the instructor had revealed that the quote was from two thousand years in the past.

Of course, Towstick told himself, things this time around do seem a bit different. Sure, maybe all generations go through the same thing, but it sure does feel worse somehow.

The young man was one of a new breed of policeman. New York City's government, like that of most large metropolitan areas, especially those along the East Coast of the country, had always been corrupt. And, from Tampa to Bangor they had uniformly possessed police forces to match. But, when Theodore Roosevelt had been chief of police in New York, he had thrown his energies into cleaning up its particularly odious taint. One of the traditions which had started with him was the hiring of college graduates, men with something more to offer the city than simply brutality and corruption.

Upon entering the modest but respectable halls of Brooklyn College, Towstick had opted for earning his degree from their School of Humanities and Social Sciences. His eventual goal had always been to join the force. His reckoning was that training in history and psychology, among others, would be his optimum way to reach it.

"And, when does this start?"

"When I called in to tell 'em we were knockin' for lunch," Brodsky answered, "the sarge said to report in when we was done. Apparently we've got our night and a lotta the next two days all mapped out for us."

"All mapped out for us, eh? Well, a bit of certainty never hurts a guy, I guess."

"I don't know," responded the older officer in a tone of mock seriousness. "What's that famous quote about being certain?"

"You mean, 'I am certain of nothing but the holiness of the heart's affections, and the truth of imagination' … that one?"

"What? No. Who the hell said that?"

"That was John Keats. What—no poetry classes on the Normandy Beach?"

"Not that I recall," responded Brodsky. Taking one of the few remaining bites of his sandwich, he spoke as he chewed;

"No, I was thinkin' more the one about there being nothin' certain in this world but death and taxes. That was Ben Franklin. I mention that because I figure you didn't have time for much American History at your fancy college. All you guys are pinkos, right?"

Towstick put up his hands in surrender. Both men smiled slightly, giving silent acknowledgement that their partnership was a comfortable one. As Brodsky sucked the mustard from the fingers of his left hand, the junior officer nodded, adding;

"Da, comrade." The comment made the senior policeman chuckle. As the two began preparing to leave their diner of choice, Towstick, feeling a need to make one final quip, threw out;

"However, I do believe Mr. Franklin, an educated man himself, might have been inspired by a previous source. The Roman scholar, Pliny the Elder, who first put it as 'the only certainty is that nothing is certain.'"

Brodsky, finished pulling bills from his wallet, looked at his partner and said with a sigh;

"You know, if my wife ever heard the shit I talk about with you, I do believe she'd accuse me of puttin' on airs."

"Well, that's what you get for hanging out with commies."

Both men chuckled, then headed for the cash register. As far as they knew, they would pay their bill, report in to the sergeant on duty at their station for details on working the Bellweather event, and then proceed to ride herd over a crowd of concerned citizens for the rest of their weekend. Simple, straight-forward—a future with the promise of little in the way of excitement or the unexpected.

All in all, the kind of comforting routine for which all those with even the slightest concept of actual chaos fervently pray for on a regular basis.

* * *

"Well, I'd say that could have gone worse."

There was truth to the thought that the first night of the reverend's rally could have gone quite differently. At several times throughout the evening more than one officer on site had feared the possibility of an outbreak of violence. Bellweather, although a slight, nearly skeletal figure of a man, could rise to the moment. Humble, quiet and withdrawn before he had taken the stage which had been erected on the beach at Coney Island for his use, once in front of his audience he became a veritable force of nature.

"Oh, no argument." Brodsky agreed with his partner emphatically. "That preacher might be scrawny, but he can sure stir up a crowd."

At a number of points during the night, Bellweather had called for an end to rock and roll, and his audience had roared in agreement. He wanted the music of the new era stripped from the airwaves, banned from both television and radio, removed even from private clubs. Condemned in every manner possible.

"It is a dark and malevolent ruination," he had intoned, "a soul-damning blasphemy unknown since the days of Sodom and Gomorrah. Understand, good people, the black and horrible truth—this sinister blight is nothing less than the catastrophic opening gambit of the forces of evil, and if it is not opposed, if it is not stopped dead in its tracks, then the floodgates shall be opened for all manner of wretched depravity and the sun will go black in the sky from the stench of the monstrous degradation and perversion which shall rise from the charnel house that once was the collective soul of mankind!"

The officers on duty had to do their best to ignore the goings on upon the stage. Their job was to watch the crowd, to control the situation. But the reverend was an unexpectedly powerful, and distracting, speaker. The amount of words he could cram into a single sentence amazed young Towstick especially.

Of course, part of the reverend's showmanship came from the staging of the event itself. Held outside, with the vastness of the Atlantic stretched out behind him, the sound of the incoming tide lapping against the shore, the venue took on a natural, honest feel. As the sun set off to the west, and massive bonfires were lit at a cue from Bellweather, the crowd was drawn in even further, especially when the preacher began to tie in the mutual threats of communism and nuclear war.

"So," the younger officer asked his partner as they stood at the connecting gate between the beach and the streets beyond, directing those leaving to keep moving in an orderly fashion, "what did you think of the good reverend now that we've had a taste of him all up-and-close?"

"He can certainly light a fire under people. I'll give him that much."

"Especially when the subject is Randy Jones."

"Yeah, you mentioned that before. Made me notice it tonight. He really don't like this Jones very much, that's for sure. Any idea why?"

"I don't know," answered Towstick. "It's not like his music is any more ... what would you call it—"

"Depraved?" Brodsky said the single word with a grin.

"Well, that's what the reverend might call it, but I mean, I've heard the Seldoms. It's just the same junk all the others are throwing out there. 'My girl's the greatest.' Then 'Boo hoo, my girl left me.' Followed by 'I'm so lucky, my new girl's so sweet.'"

Brodsky laughed to the point of choking.

"Christ, yeah..." the older officer managed to sputter. "They do sound like they're all cut pretty much from the same end of the ham, don't they?"

"I know," answered Towstick absently, nodding, watching the thinning flow of people move off to their cars or the subway station beyond. "That's why I can't figure out what's so special about Jones."

"It is a little weird," agreed Brodsky. "But that's the way of it with these guys. Could be Jones is just Bellweather's Jews." When the younger officer simply stared, not able to follow his partner's reasoning, Brodsky explained;

"You know, Hitler ... he had the Jews. They were to blame for everything. 'If only we hadn't let the Jews get Germany in such a mess. If we just take care of the Jews, everything will be fine again.' That kind of shit. You know, you find someone to blame for everything that's wrong, then you work on sellin' the rubes your cure for those ills."

Towstick nodded, unable to find fault with his partner's logic. He did not like to think of the reverend as a simple con man, but there was no denying the tactics were the same. There were few that might characterize Hitler as merely a con man, of course, but ultimately, the officer thought, that was all he had been. Just a crooked loudmouth with a sucker's message.

But, the young man asked himself, if that's the case, then just what is your message, reverend?

And, through the simple act of posing an innocent question to himself, Towstick threw his life onto a course he could never have imagined. One that no man could have ever imagined. And most certainly, one for which no man would have ever wished.

* * *

Towstick stood on the beach at Coney Island, looking about himself, fairly certain he was dreaming. For one thing, he was far closer to the reverend

at that moment than he had been earlier. Also, the ocean was burning, and that did not seem normal to him in the least.

"Fire," Bellweather's voice boomed, washing across the sand and sea, "is needed. And fire is coming. A cleansing fire is coming. And you must decide, all of you, whether you shall be in control of that inferno, or consumed by it."

Although the conflagration consuming the ocean grew more wide-spread every second, the sky went darker at the same rate. Looking up, Towstick saw the cause. All light from above was being blotted out by a blackness carpeting the sky. The officer stared for a moment, then realized it was not one vast thing, but many small ones.

"For those who merely stand to the sides, pointing their fingers, laughing at the truth, they shall be the first to be consumed by the coming terrors. But they shall not be the only ones."

Dark as fear, fanged and taloned, born on wings three times the size of the creatures themselves, the things were a boil of unorganized body parts, a mad assembly moving across the sky with no discernable purpose. What they might be, or simply symbolize within his dream, Towstick did not know. But, it took him only seconds to realize from where they were coming.

"These are the end days, as foretold a thousand times. As mentioned in every holy book, not just our own blessed Bible, but those of all religions, of all faiths. This is the final judgment, come rushing upon us. And those not prepared shall know the horrible price of their indecision."

Far out on the ocean, the officer made out the shape of a massive mushroom cloud. That, he realized, was what had set the sea ablaze. And, as he watched the cloud itself dissipate, he saw that the crumbling radioactive dust and waste was not falling to be mixed with the waves, but was reforming through some unknown agency into the flying monstrosities.

"The destroyer is coming. He is here. His legions are laying claim to the souls of the confused and the uncertain. By the hundreds of thousands he is sweeping them up, dragging them from the light and down to everlasting pain and damnation!"

Even realizing he was dreaming, Towstick felt uncomfortable. The creatures overhead were fearsome in sight and sound, their cries so terrible he had to cover his ears with his hands. Worse, though, the heat coming from the blazing ocean had him awash in sweat, his clothing sticking to him at every point of contact. Every inch of his skin soaked, his eyes burning from the contact—mouth tasting of salt.

"And the beast is moving across the face of the Earth. And you shall know the sight of him, and those whom do not believe, will not see him for what he is. But those who do know the face of evil might still be spared."

And then, looking up into the sky, Towstick saw a face forming in the glowing, ash-filled sky. Massive and all-consuming, its eyes filled with hatred and a mouth curled from a blistering greed, it came together bit by bit, all of it projecting a terrible and alien hostility, the sight of it both repelling and yet fascinating the young man until finally he recognized the visage forming above him.

He tried to turn away, but the monstrous face filled the burning sky, demanding his attention. Towstick grasped at the hope that he was asleep—merely dreaming. And then, the miles wide lips above him parted to say;

"Be seeing you..."

And young officer Towstick's dream mind shattered, leaving him screaming in his sleep.

* * *

"So, who was it?"

Towstick stared over at his partner behind the wheel of their squad car. He did not answer Brodsky at first, his mind still caught in the horror of his night. The sight of the face in the sky had left the young officer shaken. His own cries of fright had awakened him, leaving him agitated to the point where the idea of attempting to return to sleep filled him with dread.

Sticky all over, having apparently perspired as much in reality as he had within his dream, Towstick had gone to take a shower, finding something once he entered the bathroom that left him even more shaken. While dreaming, he had begun to bleed—not just from his nostrils, but from his tear ducts and gums as well.

"The face…" he muttered absently, "yeah, the face…"

Terribly frightened without knowing why, Towstick had clambered into his shower and turned the water on the hottest setting at full blast. Unable to grasp soap or washrag, he had simply turned his body slowly beneath the burning water, letting it wash away the blood and stink.

"That was the weird part…"

"Are you kiddin' me," asked Brodsky, his eyes narrowing, "atomic bombs in Coney Island, crazy bat monsters fillin' the sky, and whose face was in the sky was the weird part?"

Eventually, tired of making circles, the officer had simply lowered himself to the point where he could sit within his tub. The water pounding at him, scalding him, he had remained beneath it until the sun had shattered the darkness outside his window.

"Well, yeah … because I was, I don't know, expecting it to be the devil or something—"

"So … who was it?"

"Randy Jones."

At first, Brodsky did not answer. What, after all, could he say? So, his partner had a bad dream. A crazy dream. That kind of stuff happened.

Still, he thought, he had to say something—offer *something*. Clearing his throat, giving himself several additional seconds to think, he finally said;

"Listen, if I'd had a dream like that, I don't think I would have even said anything. Unless, hummm, you know, if I thought it meant somethin'. So, I guess I'm askin' … do you think it meant somethin'?"

"I don't know," answered the younger man as honestly as possible. "I mean, normally I wouldn't think anything of it. Just a dream, you know? But this … I don't know where it could have come from. The words I heard the reverend saying, it wasn't anything he'd said last night."

Towstick went silent again, something he had done during most of their drive. Brodsky did not push him. The older man had been an officer longer than his partner had been alive. He knew the multitude of pressures that could come to bear on police officers. Knew how they could come from seemingly nowhere to destroy a perfectly good man and his career.

"Look," said Towstick finally, "it's not like a dream can mean anything. This isn't the dark ages. Let's just get down to Coney. We've got to do our part to … to keep the reverend safe—"

"So he can destroy rock and roll."

"Yeah, I guess so."

Brodsky hit his turn signal, moving their squad car off King's Highway and onto Stillwell Avenue. Maneuvering them through several close-set red signals by using their alert lights, the older officer waited until they were in clear traffic once more, then asked;

"So when Jones shows up in the sky and sets off his A-bombs and all, do we shoot him, or call the civil defense?"

"You're a real asshole," responded Towstick, grateful for his partner's lightening the mood.

"Jeez, you try to be understandin'…"

Knowing they would be at Coney Island in a

matter of minutes, Towstick merely nodded, then shut his eyes. Jamming himself into the corner created by the front seat and the passenger side door, the younger man took a deep breath and then released it, trying to clear his mind before he had to start patrolling the gathering crowds. No matter how hard he concentrated, however, he could not rid himself of the image of a burning ocean, nor of Randy Jones' monstrous visage staring down at it approvingly.

* * *

"Heads up, partner," said Brodsky just loud enough to be heard over the sound of the reverend's loudspeaker-enhanced voice. Turning to see what the older officer had spotted, Towstick saw a stirring in the crowd roughly a hundred and fifty feet away from their position. As best he could tell, someone was moving through the throng, someone recognizable enough to cause the beginnings of a commotion.

"Any ideas?"

"Yeah," offered Brodsky. "We do our jobs."

Towstick nodded, his eyes narrowing as he scanned the area behind them, trying to ascertain who or what was causing the building commotion. It took some five minutes for the cause to reach the spot where the two officers were stationed.

"Oh," thought Towstick, "here's something no one was expecting."

Brodsky and his partner both helped clear a space as several other officers continued to help move Randy Jones forward through the crowd. Of course, word of the rocker's arrival at the rally spread from person to person far faster than the musician could make his way forward. Towstick tried to imagine how volatile the situation might become, but could make no guesses with which he was comfortable.

Certainly there were fans of Jones present, dragged along to hear the reverend by their parents. But, they were outnumbered by far by folks who either were concerned that the musician's music might be in some way harmful or who felt he was an agent of Satan sent to corrupt their children and steal their souls for Hell. The young officer's hand slid unconsciously to rest upon his weapon as the reverend's voice halted for a moment, then started anew, announcing;

"And so, the very demon of whom I speak walks into our midst. What seek you here, monster?"

"Man, you really are on the fast train headed for way-out-there, aren't you?"

Jones' voice could not be heard by the entire crowd as could the reverend's. Knowing this, Bell-weather repeated the musician's comment for the crowd. When a wave of invective was hurled at Jones in response, however, the reverend roared;

"No, I say unto you, do not fall from the path. Do not threaten or raise your fists against this man. Though he be a foul corruptor of all that is decent, still is he our brother, possessed of a soul that must be saved like any other."

"That's mighty generous, preacher," shouted Jones. "Let me just say, I didn't come here to cause you trouble. Honestly, I didn't think your crowd would recognize me, not after sundown. I just wanted to catch a glimpse of your act, is all."

"My act?" The reverend paused for a moment, then said, "you are a clever one, Mr. Jones, I will grant you that. But you are not so clever as to draw me into a war of words. Your master is the prince of twisted truths, and I am humble enough to realize I am no match for he who has dragged billion of souls off to his fiery kingdom."

"Whatever you say, preacher."

"If such is true," snapped Bellweather instantly, "then what I say unto you is, relent from your evil ways. Cease the corruption of our innocent youth. Return to the bosom of our Lord God Jesus Christ, not for my sake, not even for that of the children your presence threatens to destroy, but for your own good. For your own soul. For that only precious belonging each man holds. If what I say can actually matter to you, then I say to you, Randolf Vincent Jones … come back to the God who loves you dearly before your time runs down. Before the last grains of sand clear the glass, and you are lost forever."

Towstick watched Jones, as well as the crowd around him, his eyes darting from spot to spot. He was professional enough not to allow any part of his mind to drive him to panic. What would happen, would happen. The police, he understood—which much of the public did not—were not magicians. They could not predict crime. Their job was not so much to prevent wrongdoings, but to stand against those who committed them.

It might have been reckless for Jones to appear at the rally, but it was not a criminal act. That was the dangerous thing about free speech. The musician had certainly put himself in harm's way. All it would take was one hurled brick, coming out of the darkness and striking him in the head, to cause irreparable damage to the force. The media would report that it was the department's fault if anything happened to Jones. They would claim the police should have removed him for his own good.

Of course, to do so would be a violation of his rights. If they were to do the perfectly sensible thing and take the musician into protective custody to prevent the riot every officer in the area was dreading at that moment, they would be letting the department in for any number of lawsuits.

"Damned if you do…"

Towstick let his whispered words trail off as Jones responded to the reverend's offer.

"It's nice to think that someone cares what happens to my soul, preacher. Very nice. But I must decline. I came here, like I said, simply to see what you were all about. Now that I have, I'm not nearly as worried as I was."

"And, my dear Mr. Jones," Bellweather's voice thundered down from his makeshift pulpit, "why is that?"

"Because you are exactly what I thought you were, which is no threat at all." Ripples of angry whispers flashed through the crowd as the musician's words were repeated from person to person.

"You and your kind, you're the past, preacher. You're done. You're finished. There's a whole big world full of new ideas out there, and your kind, frightened by anything you don't understand, there's no room for you here anymore."

"You are a sad, doomed creature, Mr. Jones," answered Bellweather. As the musician shook his head and turned away, walking back toward the games and rides of the Coney Island boardwalk, the reverend bellowed;

"Many have set themselves up as being something more than our Lord, and they all are dust in their graves, forgotten at best, reviled at worst. You shall not outlast the one, true Christ. You are at best an annoying thorn in His side, a lost soul for whom He shall weep, as He does for any who lose the struggle for eternal happiness. But that is all your actions will profit you, good sir, pain, suffering, and eternal damnation. And nothing more."

"We shall see, preacher," called out Jones as he drew close to the place where Towstick had been stationed. "We shall see."

After that exchange, Bellweather returned to speaking to his spectators, exhorting them to allow the musician safe passage and to learn from his example the dangers of pride. As the tension in the air began to fade, Towstick felt himself suddenly awash with relief. During the exchange between the reverend and Jones, every officer present had prepared for the worst. Now that they could feel the moment passing, they all began to relax—at least a bit.

None were as relieved as Towstick, however. The young officer had never before been in such a volatile position, where it would have taken no more than a single spark to ignite a riot the police could never have controlled. As he watched Jones make his way through the crowd, part of Towstick's mind was thanking Bellweather for handling things in such a reasonable and calm manner while another tried to determine just what the musician thought he might accomplish by showing up in the first place.

And then, something happened to throw all of Towstick's thoughts aside. As Jones drew closer, retracing his earlier path, he came within several feet of the officer and suddenly stopped. Turning his head, he made eye contact with Towstick, and then said just loud enough for the officer to hear;

"Be seeing you."

And Towstick's eyes went wide, even as his hand once more went unconsciously to the butt of his weapon.

* * *

After the rally, Towstick had begged off going out for a beer with Brodsky, wanting—needing—to be alone. At home he had done his own drinking, downing far more than he would have with his partner. Halfway through a fifth of bourbon, a bottle which had sat unopened in his cupboard since his father had given it to him two Christmases earlier, the officer realized he was—for lack of a better term—medicating himself.

"Heh," he had laughed at himself, "afraid to go to bed now, are we?"

"No," answered a voice from deep within his brain, "afraid to dream."

As the thought passed through his mind, the young man found his hands shaking, each breath coming more rapidly. Pulling himself together, he screwed the cap back on his bottle, returned it to its place in his cupboard, and then headed for his shower. On the way he sat down on his living room couch to think for a moment. Before his spine had finished settling in to the cushioned back, he was already asleep.

* * *

"Okay, so you look like hell."

Towstick only nodded. Alcohol had not stopped him from dreaming. If anything, he felt he had prolonged the terror by putting himself into a stupor from which he could not awaken. His nightmare had begun with the same images from the night previous, but then had moved through a series of escalating horrors. All around Towstick, the world had fallen into ever more degenerate shambles. Blood in the streets, cities on fire, lovers in despair, children abandoned by the millions, babies slaughtered by their own mothers … more.

He had beheld a hundred thousand terrible images, all of which he somehow *knew* were a part of his own future. When his own screams had finally shocked him to consciousness, he had staggered to his shower. Turning the water to its most scalding, he had crumpled into the steam and heat and sobbed.

"You gonna be all right for work?"

"Yeah, sure," Towstick had grunted. "Let's just get this shit over with."

Brodsky had given his partner a sideways glance, but had then shrugged and simply slid into the driver's seat of their squad car. Towstick had rested with his head against the window frame through the entire ride to Coney Island. As the last night of the rally had proceeded, he had stood his watch with a look so distracted those who noticed wondered if he might be in some way ill. When the event finally finished for the evening, a grateful Towstick was more than ready to leave. His only thoughts of trying to sleep. To rest. In blessed dreamlessness for once. Before Brodsky could pull away, however, one of the reverend's assistants approached their vehicle, requesting a moment.

"The good Reverend heard of an officer who may have fallen ill in his service," the man said quickly, his face aimed at Brodsky, his eyes on Towstick—

"He also heard that the young man had complained of dreams, terrible nightmares … involving a certain musician—"

Both officers remembered the moment when they had first left their squad car, when Towstick had confided to his partner about the details of his dreams. Each strained to remember the crowd around them, who might have even had the opportunity to have heard so much. And, they did both *know* that was the moment in question.

Towstick knew he had told no one other than his partner, and that Brodsky would never have said anything to anyone. Not without at least telling him. As for Brodsky, he knew his partner. Knew the younger man would come to him with a problem before he would tell anyone else.

"The Reverend would very much like to speak with this young man … if at all possible. He feels it might be very important."

Something in the man's voice caught both their ears.

"Where?"

The assistant smiled gratefully, handing Brodsky a card while he said;

"73rd … just off the park to the west. The Reverend is being taken there now."

Brodsky cast his eyes at his partner, caught Towstick's barely perceptible nod, then answered;

"Well, let's not keep him waitin'."

* * *

"Come in, Officer Towstick," said the reverend, sitting on a couch in the living room of his suite. Turning to his aide on duty, he said, "George, why don't you take Officer Brodsky downstairs for some refreshment." Turning back to Towstick, he said;

"I believe we might need to talk in private for at least a while."

Once the pair were alone, Bellweather asked his guest about his dreams. Somewhat uncomfortable at first, the reverend's open, attentive manner soon had Towstick telling the story of his nightmares without hesitation. He told Bellweather everything, not certain what good it might do, but feeling more relieved with each word simply for having done so. When he finished, Towstick saw that the reverend was sitting back, eyes closed, fingers intertwined, hands resting on his stomach. Without moving, or opening his eyes, Bellweather asked;

"Did you know the Nazis were actually working on the atomic bomb before we were?" When the officer admitted he did not, the reverend continued, telling him;

"Oh, yes. Well on their way. And then, suddenly, they dropped that line of research—moved off into other things. And, at the same time, we started our development of an atomic bomb here. Why do you think that was?"

"I … I don't know."

"Because we couldn't allow the Nazis to win the war." As Towstick blinked, staring in utter confusion, Bellweather said;

"There is a storm coming, but of a magnitude you cannot imagine. The Nazis would have used nuclear bombs to subjugate and control the world. Such weapons would have been an iron leash with which they would have directed the planet—and mankind—forward. And, a unified humanity, led by a determined body politic with an iron will … no, we couldn't have that."

"Reverend," asked Towstick, his confusion

practically overwhelming, "I don't understand. Who's 'we?'"

"*We,* officer, are beyond your understanding. *We* have directed the progress of your existence from when you were but slime bubbling in a fetid swamp. And *we* have no intention of halting our guidance until you are what we desire."

Towstick wanted to simply get up and leave. Fears he could not explain clawed at him, shrieking within his mind, howling at him to run away and never look back. Paralyzed, however, half by curiosity, half by terror, he remained.

"We knew the Allies, needing to think of themselves as … good…" Bellweather said the word with a patronizing chuckle, "would use restraint. That was why we whispered in the ears of the Nazis, misdirected them to other directions. We needed a free world, one living under a never-ending threat of destruction, to prepare you for the final steps."

Towstick opened his mouth, but found he could not speak. Sensing his questions, the reverend said;

"The Axis powers believed in forging mankind into the best it could be. We had no use for that. We need a chaotic, scattered humanity. And that is where America will take the world. We have always sifted through the possible futures before you, making adjustments as best we can—"

"As best…"

"Our reach into your plane is … limited, for now. Unable to act freely, we must use puppets. Such as," Bellweather pointed to himself, "the reverend here. Or yourself. Or…"

As Bellweather paused, the door to the suite opened. As someone entered the foyer, the reverend's voice sounded;

"Ah, our final marionette strides forth."

Towstick managed to turn his head enough to watch as Randy Jones entered the room. The young man threw himself onto the couch next to the officer, saying;

"Don't sweat it, man. Don't try and make sense of it."

"But, I … my dreams…"

"Merely your mind trying to understand that which had touched it. We could not bend you without revealing somewhat of the direction into which your vision would be thrust." Bellweather smiled, spreading his hands before him as he explained;

"Already men are planning to spread out into the solar system, then the galaxy beyond. We cannot have that. The Nazis would have been on the moon by now. And your kind will most likely reach that one satellite, but that will be all."

"You see," said Jones, "the time is coming when we'll be able to enter your world without any difficulty. But, by your reckoning, it's still, sixty, seventy years off. We can't have you getting off planet, building energy weapons, getting organized. We need you to remain as you've always been—greedy, at each other's throats, vainly chasing your own self-interest."

Towstick slammed his eyes closed, forcing their lids together as tightly as possible. His mind spinning, he desperately tried to make sense of all he was hearing, even as Bellweather said;

"Soon, your churches will be empty. As the intellectual classes destroy 'God,' the masses, left with nothing in which to believe, will drown themselves in an endless parade of diversions. Cults, drugs, a hundred thousand vanities will follow. Women will murder their unborn children simply to avoid stretch marks."

"B-But…" Towstick stammered, "w-why?"

"As life loses meaning, its opposite becomes more attractive."

His eyes still closed, fists pressed against his face, the young officer screamed;

"But I don't understand!"

"And," Jones' voice sounded in his ear, "you don't need to. You simply have to play your part."

"My … part?"

"You need to arrest the reverend," answered the musician, standing, walking away from the couch.

Towstick was about to question Jones' words when the sound of gunfire forced his eyes open. As he stared, mouth agape, eyes unblinking, he saw the singer's body fly backwards, smashing its way through the window beyond. Shaking his head, he twisted it about quickly, finding Bellweather approaching him, the weapon he had used to slay the musician held out before him."

"Disarm me, officer. It's your duty."

* * *

Of course, Towstick never spoke of what had been said to him in the reverend's suite to anyone. He did as Bellweather instructed, saying that Jones had come at the reverend's invitation, and been murdered without warning. Bellweather had spoken of a need for disruption, for disillusionment—more. Towstick had not heard him. Or at least, had not retained any of what he had said.

Bellweather was not a major figure, nor had been Jones. New York had done everything within its power to minimize the story, as had been expected. But it was enough. Over the following months, Towstick would be forgotten by the world, but the tale he had been groomed to tell would spread. Distrust of authority would spread with it. Rebellion would follow, but of the most infantile, self-aggrandizing type. The coming decades would pass, and the possible greatness of mankind would be reduced to a collective fretting over the most ridiculous of banalities.

Comfortable within the back of Towstick's mind, as it had been, and was, within so many others, the Chaos watched futures unfold through a thousand sets of eyes across a multitude of dimensions.

There were, it thought, so many messages to be delivered. Quite pleased with the directions set into motion, realizing the desired futility of purpose had been all but assured, it turned its attention elsewhere.

After all, the race it had just doomed to sputter off into a useless clamoring after empty insanities was by no means all that important. The 'Earth,' as Towstick's mind labeled it, was but a lost and tiny mudball on the furthest reaches of its galaxy. A trifle. A nothing.

There were far more important worlds requiring its attention. And, so thinking, the Chaos slithered forth from the young officer's mind, leaving him to desperately try to remember why he had ever felt important. Abandoning him to nothing more than a future of meaningless continuation, piling up one useless moment atop another.

Finally, of course, the weight of it all would crush him under its futility and then alcohol, or a well-aimed bullet, would snuff out his ridiculously brief existence. Which, in the Chaos' opinion, as he departed Towstick's mind, leaving the officer with nothing but silence, was all the vulgar noise known as humanity deserved.

The London Necropolis Railway

From the glass roof where no shadow falls,
from cool, arched, glazed London brick viaduct,
from lavish-wrought iron gates opening like a mouth,
from a temple to the modern.
The train in insistent steam departs.
Moves on.

Walk with softest step along narrow corridors.
Watch through the bevelled window
a bubble frozen in the pane.
The mourners jolting to the rhythm of the Necropolis
        Train
are a puzzle needing completion,
a missing piece, buried in your mind's memorium.
Move on.

No coin pressed against your tongue.
No taste of copper in your parched mouth.
You have no obol for the ferryman.
Instead you clutch the coffin ticket for
your third class funeral.
Move on.

Here's a lady dressed in lace as delicate as her
breathless face. So still, she watches
the children crying, unsoothed by the nurse maid,
or their silent father.
She joins you.
Move on.

Here's a man, a likely fella
You might have met him down the docks
shared a drink, a laugh.
There are no words left to be said.
He joins you.
Move on.

Here are silent twins, old men
dressed in rags or silk, street women
still smelling of the Thames,
shrouded girls and worn-faced men.
Move on. Move on.
There are no words to be said
Move along the dark corridors, the vastly swelling
        hoard.

You who never travelled beyond the Bells.
Leaving all behind.
It was a good life,
yet you shrug it off like a worn coat.
No tears or grief.
All is past.
There is no emotion for the dead.
Move on.
Take this journey from Waterloo Bridge Station.
Take the London Necropolis to the Green Country.

— Kelda Crich

Runnin'

Story by Steven J. Bitz
Illustration by Paul Niemiec

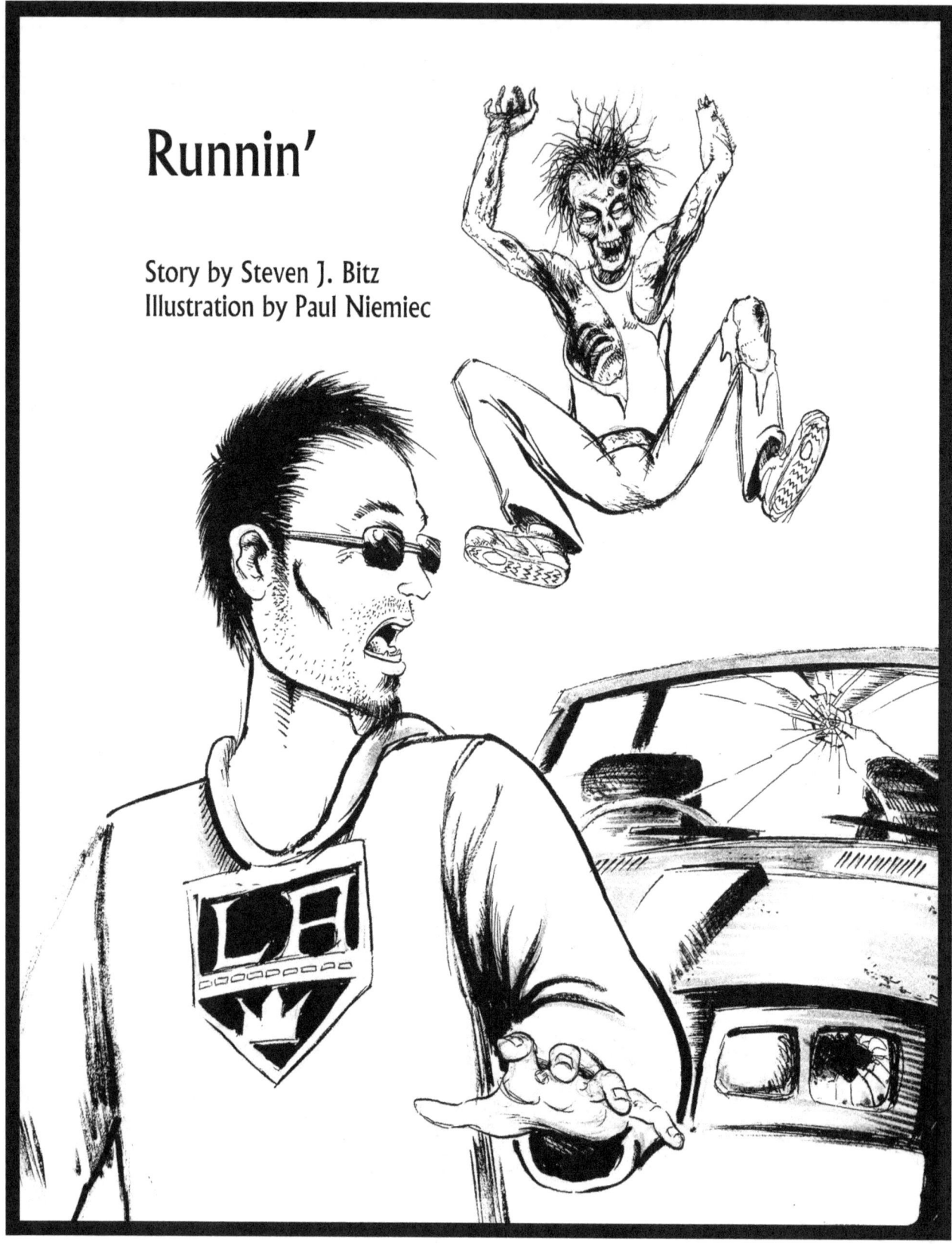

My feet pound across the concrete, shredding the placid silence that engulfs Los Angeles like a funeral shroud. I flinch as bright sunlight gleams from an abandoned Starbuck's shattered window. Trying to avoid the mess, I leap forward, but my shoes still crunch across the layer of broken g1ass. I cross the street, swerving around a cart and approach the edge of my territory. It won't be much longer till I have to expand, as I've scavenged nearly every useful bit so far.

On the other side of the street, I head toward an alley cloaked in shadows. I slow a mite before entering, eyes dart in for any sign of danger, then pour on the speed. It's always kinda comforting, knowing the shadows hide my presence from searching eyes, and sorta thrilling 'cause I can't always see what might be hiding from me in turn.

My slapping shoes echo around me as I speed toward the opening at the far end. 'Bout halfway there, I start to get a creepy feelin' that whispers, "You're being watched," in a singsong, playground taunting kinda way. I hastily glance at the gaping openings above but don't see anyone peering down. Just nerves, I guess.

My imagination chases me the rest of the way down the alley until I burst free. Sunlight bathes me, knocking the oppressive little monkey from my shoulder, and a grin stretches across my face. I swerve into the middle of the street and proceed with my hunt for supplies.

PAD, pad, PAD, pad, PAD, pad. My shoes continue to echo behind me, each step rebounding in my ears.

After a brief moment, I realize there aren't any walls close enough to create that sorta echo, not even in this mausoleum of a city. I look behind me and catch sight of a runner keepin' pace. I slow a bit, hoping he'll maybe catch up. It's been a long while since I've had a friend.

As he nears, I see that he sports a pair of cut-off jeans and a black T-shirt. I see his head bobbing wildly from side-to-side. *Huh, that's kinda weird.* I look closer and see the ragged wound in the right side of his neck.

Crap on a stick.

I take off so fast I woulda been flying down the block if only I coulda grown wings. I run around a cluster of vehicles at an old crash site and across another street. He speeds up and follows, keeping pace.

There's no way he shoulda done that.

You see, the thing about zombies is, they're pretty much the same as when they were alive. They can do the same things, even if they are a little slow in the head. They're not stronger or faster, like you mighta seen in one of them old movies.

The poor guy—or gal, I'm not sexist—mighta been faster than me at one time, but gettin' bit by a zombie is pretty much the same as getting' gnawed on by a pack of wild dogs. When the newly risen undead gets going, there usually ain't much left. I don't care how fast you were before the feast; a half-chewed calf muscle or a missin' hunk of thigh tends to put a damper on your speed.

I run faster and take a quick peek back. He does too—the run faster part, that is—head really flopping around. Doesn't seem to affect his runnin' ability much. Obviously, I'm dealing with a zombie who'd run before gettin' dead and all those old instincts are still very much alive and kickin', so to speak.

I tear off down another street, heading to an abandoned lot I know about. He's a determined sucker, 'cause he stays with me the whole way. I finally see the place a minute later, and grin.

A six-foot high chain link fence surrounds what used to be a private parking area. A few abandoned cars are scattered throughout the lot, but that's not why I've come here.

Sprinting the last hundred yards, I slow near the end then leap up and grab the top of the fence. Scrambling over, I land on the other side. I stumble a few more feet, then turn to face my shadow.

Zombies have a hard time with fences. 'Specially fences they can see through. They can see you, but they ain't smart enough to figure out how to get you. I've seen 'em spend hours banging against a fence trying to get at what's on the other side. Hey, with no TV, where do you think I get my entertainment?

As this guy approaches, he doesn't slow at all. I cringe, expecting the crash, but that doesn't happen. At the last moment, he leaps, latching onto the top of the fence, and pulls up his legs like some sorta fence hoppin' freak. He clears the obstacle in one bound, far more gracefully than I'd done.

Well if that don't just beat all, a Goddamned parkour Zombie.

As Parkour lands, one arm lashes out and he tries to snatch me with a clawed hand. It's like one of them action movies where time slows to a crawl. I see the ragged ends of his fingernails, and the dried blood staining the creases. The second joint of his middle finger ends in a mangled stump like the butt of a mashed, chewed cigar. His fingers pass within an inch of my face as I lean away just in time.

I fall back two steps to keep my balance, but by then I'm well outta Parkour's grasp. I turn back to the fence I'd just climbed over and everything kinda rushes back to normal all in one big whoosh of color and sound.

I bound three steps and jump. My left foot smashes into the fence and I push off. Surging up, my right foot lands on top. Then I pull my left leg over and drop to the other side. It's not pretty, and it's sure as hell not Parkour, but it gets the job done.

I catch a glimpse of Parkour as I land. He's already recovered from my near-death experience and heading my way. I don't wait to see what he'll do—fool me once and all that—I just run.

My heart pounds as I sprint away. It's a good thing I'd run these streets before, 'cause all I can think about is how Parkour's teeth woulda felt if he'd caught me.

Every nerve in my body surges. A wave of heat courses through me, then a cold shock like the one I got that time I jumped off the pier into the ocean. I feel each muscle flex, every swish of fabric across my body, the caress of wind along my skin. I feel alive, like one of those fools that jumps outta perfectly good airplanes.

My eyes dart around, latching onto bright spots of color: The azure sky above, a yellow curtain fluttering from a third-story window, a purple flower bursting from a patch of weeds. I keep waiting for one of them to turn into a zombie and eat a few others, but it ain't happened yet.

My ears catch a trill of birdsong, but the rapid echo of my own steps draws my attention. I glance over my shoulder.

Parkour dogs my trail, head bobbing tike an eager puppy, one far too willing to sink his teeth into me.

I pour on more speed, running so fast my feet scratch across the sidewalk. My shoes can't get enough traction on the dirty surface, so I slow a bit, making sure to stay ahead of Parkour.

Doorways and windows flash past on my left, decapitated parking meter poles and abandoned cars on my right. I rapidly close the distance to the next intersection where a massive pile-up blocks the streets.

Darting through a gap between the cars, I pace onto the blacktop. I make it to the edge of the wreckage and jump onto a hood. One, two steps and I'm off, flying through the air. I absorb the impact on bent knees and duck under the bed of a semi's trailer. Rounding one massive wheel, I grab its edge and jerk to a halt. Quietly gasping air, I peer through a gap between the semi's tires.

Parkour follows, although I can't tell if he's looking for me or if his head is just wobbling like crazy. He arrives at the first car and jumps. Both feet thrust before him, Parkour barely touches his hands to the hood as he sails over the rusted hulk. He lands on the other side in a crouch, then stands and scans the wreckage.

Most of the vehicles are pretty much undamaged, but they've been trapped by others in a giant metal and grass jigsaw puzzle. That makes for lotsa places I coulda hid.

Parkour shuffles into the mess, torso swivelin' back and forth. Every few steps, his head tilts to the right, then straightens. He makes plenty of noise as he searches: banging into cars, feet scraping, occasionally grunting or letting loose with a zombie growl.

He circles around the semi and I duck-walk under the bed to the other side. I spot a woman's shoe and pick it up. It's pink and has a real long, pointy heel.

Parkour continues searching, slowly edging further from my hideaway. He grows more frantic the longer it takes to find me. The bangs, grunts, and growls come more often.

I wait until I can't see him anymore, then stand and chuck the shoe as hard as I can. It doesn't go as far as I'd like, not being made for throwing, and plops onto a vehicle down the way. Sure does make a racket though, pinging across the metal.

Parkour falls quiet. Then he charges in that. direction, unleashing the zombie equivalent of "I've got you now!' which sorta sounds like, "Aarrrr!"

As he moves away, I get a look at his back. His shirt hangs in shreds. Gaping wounds are scattered across his flesh, but none of them are really deep. Mounds of muscle ripple along his spine as he darts around the wreckage. Parkour musta had some friends around when he was bit, 'cause undisturbed zombies don't leave that much meat behind.

I'm on edge again, nerves blazing, but I don't wanna take the chance of him spotting me. I don't mind runnin' from him, but I haven't eaten for a couple of days and that alone will finish me. Soon as my adrenaline runs out, my legs'll be useless as naked sheep on shearing day.

Parkour moves outta my sight but continues to bang around for a bit. Then everything falls quiet.

I wait, holding my breath. I swivel my head, trying to pinpoint the tiniest sound. After a slow count of thirty, I suck air and rise from my crouch.

"Aarrr!"

I book it.

Parkour crashes into the semi behind me, shaking the whole damn thing with the impact.

I thread my way among the vehicles, darting into one open car, and scramble out the other side.

Parkour follows faster than I'd like. Feet clanging off bumpers, trunks and hoods, he closes the gap.

I glance back as Parkour reaches the car I'd passed through. He leaps, turning in mid-air, and slides across the roof on one hip.

That shit ain't fair.

I clear the wreckage and dart along sunset Boulevard. Huffing air, I run, my heart thudding so much it feels fit to bust from my chest.

My only advantage is speed. Parkour might be faster over and around obstacles, but so far he can only match, not exceed, my pace. I swerve back onto the sidewalk, avoiding another pile-up of abandoned vehicles—damned things are everywhere—and kick on more speed.

BOOM! A gunshot. blasts from inside a store to my left. The bullet punches a finger-sized hole in a truck along the street. I run on, hoping to hear another shot, but my left ear is ringing something fierce.

I peek. Parkour doesn't stop. He isn't blown away.

Damn.

Just before I turn the next corner, Peg Leg steps into my path. I slam my feet down, sliding and swerving another four feet before I finally change direction and hit the blacktop. It takes him a second to lock onto me, but I'm not troubled 'cause we've already met.

Peg Leg is a sight to behold. Like most zombies, he ain't much worried about personal hygiene. He wears a dirty pair of overalls covered with all manner of dried stains and rotting clumps. His left leg, from below his hip to just above his knee, is a rotted, nearly fleshless stump of exposed bone connected by a few desiccated tendons. He drags that leg behind him like a—well, you know. Even on his best day, Peg Leg's no match for me.

He hobbles toward me, reaching out with clawed fingers. His jaws gape open, long strings of saliva dripping from his teeth. A strange hissing sound issues from his mouth.

I'm used to his normal zombie growl, so this kinda catches my attention. A ragged slash spreads across his throat, the edges fluttering with passing air.

I guess whoever did that failed Zombie 101 'cause about the only thing zombies got going for 'em is they don't feel any pain. You can kick the crap outta one from here to eternity and if you ain't doing real damage they just get right. back up again. Wish I coulda seen that fella's smug face when he made that cut and Peg Leg just kept on coming. Gotta try harder than that if you wanna dead a zombie.

I arc around him, well beyond his reach, then return to the sidewalk. Parkour brushes by Peg Leg and they musta done one of them weird zombie mind-meld things 'cause Peg Leg actually leaves off chasing me and heads toward a yappy little dog on the other side of the street. If I hadn't had Parkour on my trail, I mighta tried for it myself. That mutt woulda made a decent meal. I'm kinda hoping Parkour leaves off for the easy meat too, but no such luck.

Another block on, my steps start to wobble. I push myself just to get one foot in front of the other. The air thickens around me. My lungs burn with each ragged breath. I look back.

Parkour still follows me, head bobbling like crazy. Maybe I'll get lucky and it'll just flop off.

Ha, fat chance.

I stop running, but don't stop moving. I slide another six feet to the end of the block, one leg thrust forward for balance, and change direction. Then I get back in gear.

Parkour explodes from around the corner behind me. He takes a wider turn, heading toward a van in the street. I wait for the impact, heart soaring, but he just keeps on runnin'.

Plock, plock, plock. Three steps, parallel to the ground. Just like that, he changes direction and is back on my trail.

I feel like I've been running in circles for hours. I look around, trying to get my bearings. A bit of familiar graffiti catches my eye. *The living rule - Zombies drool,* is scrawled across a boarded-up door. Below that, some joker had written, *A lot.*

Just above a pair of one-story buildings, I catch a glimpse of the Hollywood sign. Long ago, some enterprising tagger had strategically blacked-out. the old letters, so now it reads:

WE L C O ME TO T H E
Z O M BIE   A P OCA LYP SE

I know where I am.

I slow down a bit and slam my hand down on each car I pass. "Hey," I scream out between gasps. "Come … and get … it!"

Eyes darting with each step, my vision blurs as pain pounds through me. I'm not gonna make it too much longer. I continue slowing my pace and glance back. Parkour closes the gap. Then I hear what I've been waiting for.

"Eeerrrr."

Emo lumbers from a doorway down the block. Over six feet of sheer bulk, he wears tight. black jeans and a *My Dying Bride* T-shirt. A metal studded leather belt, boots, and wristbands complete his ensemble. Twin trails of dried blood and mascara tears drip below the dark caverns where his eyes used to be.

I've never been so happy to see a zombie in my whole life. I run straight for Emo. As I near, he reaches two meaty arms in my direction.

Parkour continues to close, now only a few feet behind.

"Eeerrr," Emo growls in front of me.

"Aaarrr," Parkour growls behind me.

"Screw … you, " I pant between them. Then I scream as I dodge around Emo's left side.

Emo reaches for me. Parkour follows, fingers tugging on my shirt.

Normally, zombies don't go for each other. They prefer the livin'. I know that. Parkour knows that. Emo knows that.

Emo can't see.

I make like a turtle, scrunching my head low as Emo swings one arm around. Parkour slams right into it about chest level. I hear the meaty impact. I hear Parkour crash into the ground, a loud thwack followed by another, quieter splot.

I don't know what that was. I can imagine, though, after seein' the way his head was flopping. I don't look back, I just run. Hell, these days it seems as if I'm always runnin'

You see, in the zombie apocalypse there's only one rule for survival: You don't gotta be faster than the zombies, you just gotta be faster than your friends.

'Course, If you're like me, you soon run outta friends. 'Cause damn, I'm fast. Ain't no zombie gonna ever get me. Not even a fresh one.

Night Moves

She makes her way home
over the damp bricks
of a deserted sidewalk.
Fog hangs low beneath
heavy humid air.

The click-click of her high heels
echoes in the quiet black night.
Slowly she is aware of
heavy footstep behind her.

She quickens her unescorted pace
but she feels his eyes upon her.
He is drawing near.

Mute with panic she feels
She is drowning in the thick English mist.
Only darkened shops and alleyways
loom ahead.

Without warning, a hand
grasps her shoulder, tuning her around.
Momentarily relieved by a familiar face
she breathes.

The last thing she sees
is his widening smile.
Revealing long glistening fangs
moving in for the kill.

— Louise Webster

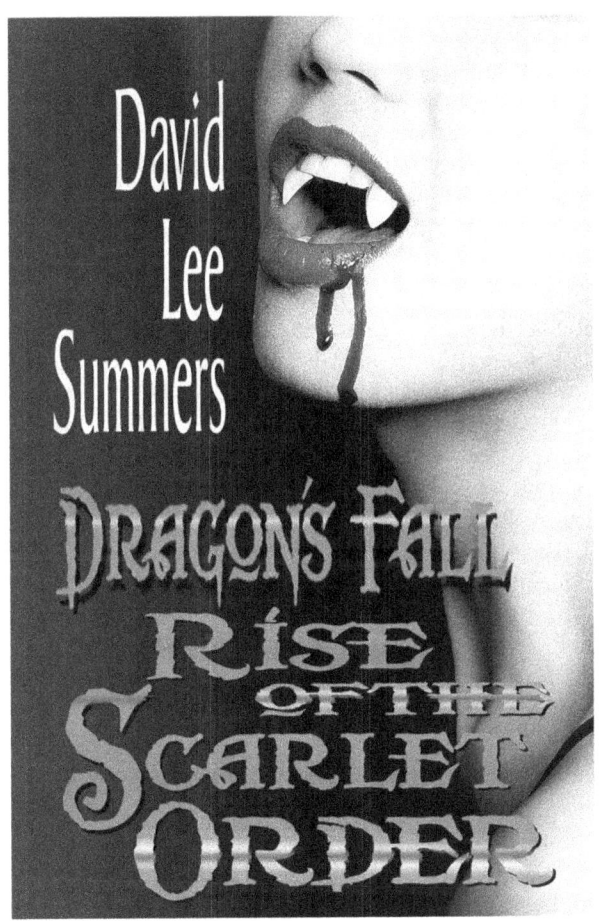

The Mirror at Delphi—An Interview With Adam Browne

Article by Robert E. Porter

The first story I read by Adam Browne had to do with Beowulf, and if you're at all familiar with Browne's writing you know what I mean; when he takes on a fictional or historical character, as he did more recently with Cyrano de Bergerac, it's a point of departure, and you're in for a very strange trip. Beowulf stepped out of an old poem, de Bergerac was a poet, and Browne writes SF or speculative poetry. This "revelation" should come as no surprise, though Browne writes in paragraph form and his work has always passed for fiction. If he had hacked the stories up and submitted the pieces as free verse, SF and speculative poetry editors would snatch these gems from the slush. But while those editors and their readers couldn't fail to recognize his language and imagery as poetic, they'd miss out on the Brownian evolution of his characters and themes, as well as the larger scope and interlocking structure of his longer narratives, because we have so often relegated SF/speculative poetry to filler, and this has left little room or regard for the epic.

If Homer, Dante, or Milton were alive today and he wanted a substantial audience for his poetry, he'd turn—like Ray Bradbury, Tim Pratt, and Adam Browne—to "prose" fiction; children's books and musicals being the only viable alternatives, and who takes them seriously? Maybe it's telling, but Browne's next project is a picture book. Browne is more fun and funnier than Milton, as I'm sure you'll agree, and he is a much better illustrator.

He lives in Melbourne, Australia, and his credits include "Space Operetta," a short story later animated as *The Adjustable Cosmos*. His first novel, *Pyrotechnicon*, was published by Coeur de Lion in 2013.

Like his friend John Dixon, who brought out his first novel—*Phoenix Island*—in January and served as consultant for the CBS show it inspired, Adam Browne is a very busy man. I'm so glad that he—and Dixon, as you'll see in the sidebar—took the time to answer my questions in Feb-April, 2014:

* * *

Robert E. Porter: What's new?

Adam Browne: Here you go - see attachment:
He sent me "Henrietta." Here's an excerpt:

Bergs like compactions of darkness, trillion-carat scarps shining dirty black in the bathysphere's lights—spongiform Henry Moore battlements, the waves of the inner core splashing up between them, slow quicksilver surges multiplying the glories of the bergs, the Ritz-big diamonds, whose roots sank in twists and whimsies as if to emblematise the strangeness below.

Pressure at 32 million times sealevel.

REP: Which came first, your art or your writing? How did you get started in visual art?

AB: Art came first. Funny how the word has contracted to mean just drawing/painting/sculpture—the word 'apple' did the same thing; at first all fruits were apples.

Anyway, drawing came first. It just came. From the same place that knowing how to build webs comes to spiders. But my childhood drawings always had a sort of narrative behind them, the way kids' drawings often are: almost always a spaceship drifting through some place more interesting than mere outerspace—often the backgrounds were vaguely biological—ramifying strands, like micrographed neurons—*Fantastic Voyage* was an influence, I think. But also a love of weirdness. It came naturally; I saw *Fantastic Planet* when very young, and it clicked with me instantly.

Presently the stories built up a head of steam and at last had to come out as text. I'm a natural draftsman, not a natural writer; but in both cases there was always a lot of anxiety, accounting for the highly detailed nature of both forms—the horror vacui of the Rococo movement, of schizophrenic artists—forever fussing until it feels right, or at least finished. I think of my stories and novels as lace that I've almost died to make. A good friend compared my stories to Faberge eggs, highly ornate but simple in form; a beautiful metaphor I think.

REP: Are you more at home with language or imagery? Which would you rather go out and explore?

AB: There are natural writers, I think, and natural visual artists; I've met one or two of the former—unfortunately, I'm the latter—being human, and therefore perverse, I want to eschew the drawing for the writing. Writing is nobler, I reckon. Or maybe it's just harder. There's a character in one of Kurt Vonnegut's lesser books who pursues painting even though he's not good at it, because 'it's his Everest'. Perversity! Distrust of the easy!

REP: Why did you want to do a picture book? How is/are *The Tame Animals of Saturn*?

AB: The title is borrowed from a chapter in Jakob Lorber's book on Saturn. Lorber was a 19th Century Austrian who was given to hear God's voice from the region of his heart: he transcribed the voice in a sort of automatic writing, producing many thousands of pages telling of various matters, including the animals and plants and geographical features of the planets. We learn about the Bisorhiohiohio fish, 18000 feet long, with its spherical head and double tongue, and the 600 foot tall Gliuba tree, whose flowers are such that 'Solomon in all his glory would pale at the sight'. His writing is outrageous and beautiful, and I'm enjoying writing about him and illustrating his creatures: I should add that the book was in part funded by friends and family through a crowdfunding campaign—I'm very grateful to everyone who contributed—it always sort of surprises me when people show belief in me, but also I think they were interested in the project itself—Lorber! What a guy! That someone hasn't made a book like this before is strange in itself! His work is so rich!—the rings of Saturn being high-water marks, as it were, indicating the size of the planet when it was larger—the planet's native name: 'Earth Calmness, World Nothingdom'—the giant butterflies hunted for their huge compound eyes by lighter-than-air children, the eyes later drained of their fluid and made into reticule handbags—the mud, a species of pig larger than mountains, which is cleanly in its habits, and digs 600 foot deep holes for the deposition of its feces—the giant snail lined with ten-pound diamonds and rubies and alabaster shell...

And so on.

It's so much fun. I'd like to visit Lorber's Saturn; not complaining about the real Saturn—would like to visit it too—but Lorber's Saturn—what fun!

REP: What does "perfection" mean to you—in writing? in art? How do you try to achieve that perfection?

AB: That's such a good question; I'm aware of my perfectionism, but have never looked at it. What does it mean? Let's start with the perfect paragraph: the prose has to be concise, but also rococo; it has to be honest, but not confessional or cathartic; it has to be clever, but never clever clever; it has to be impressive without consciously trying to impress; it has to be novel, but not outrageous; it has to contain observations from life, but not didactic; it has to be witty, but not at the expense of the several other more important layers of the writing that are balanced in slippery stacks above it; it has to contain

John Dixon discusses Adam Browne

Robert E. Porter: What was it like working with Adam?

John Dixon: Working with Adam is a blast. He's one of my favorite writers, so it's a treat to meld imaginations with him. He wows me every time. It's really a magical friendship. We started coauthoring on a lark—I think I'd mentioned wanting to write a fun and funny sci fi story reminiscent of old movies like *Angry Red Planet*—and we tumbled in, brains-first, no planning, no rules, nothing ... a great time that we've since replicated several times, generating hundreds of pages that blend our styles and concepts so completely that even we can't tell, once they're finished, who wrote what. The thing is, we love each other's brains, our egos never come into play—nothing is sacred ... least of all, us—and we always keep fun in the driver's seat.

REP: Anything you learned from the experience that you applied to your own (solo) writing?

JD: I've learned a lot from writing with Adam, who's one of the best wordsmiths in the world. He also has a gift for structural rhythm, and he nails endings. Additionally, I've learned, when stepping away from our collaborations, to embrace my differences, too, and to leverage those strengths while targeting what's fundamentally a very different market.

REP: Any chance you'll be working with Adam again?

JD: We'll definitely collaborate again—and hopefully soon. We have two nearly-finished novellas and a whole gallery of characters and ideas clamoring for release.

the minimum/maximum number of nonsubmersible elements, as Kubrick called them; it has to play with syntax, but in a way that's psychologically true; it has to be dramatic, but not overly so; it has to let the reader know what's happening in the briefest, most interesting way possible, without being terse; it has to flow.

Then comes the next paragraph, and the ones after; and I look back at them and see that this or that paragraph, once perfect by itself, is no longer so in its new context; so I go back and remove a word, shift a semicolon; replace the word; add a new idea—remove the idea, then add it, then remove it and a week later think of a whole new idea that makes the chapter work much more funly; I whip it into the text and realize that this changes something elsewhere in the novel; but that's fine—I make the change—which shifts the rhythm or whatever of a sentence or something; so I have to fix that too.

Of course, none of it is ever perfect. Perfectionist—a slightly misleading term for a person for whom nothing is ever perfect.

REP: In the early days of Andre Breton's surrealism, the first draft was IT. To revise was to tamper with genius. How many years did you spend writing and rewriting your Cyrano de Bergerac novel? Was the first draft more or less "surreal"—dreamlike, or hallucinatory—than the final, published version? You also provided illustrations for that novel. Are they more or less "surreal" than the text?

AB: Yes, what Breton did was very valuable, but he and his work were partly a product of their time; a reaction to the uptight arseholishness that presided over the late 19th Century. I remember reading an article in some 19th century magazine recounting how a young painter asked his senior how he mixed his colours: 'With care, young man, with care!'—bastard moustachios wrinkling with old man rat disdain and harrumphal superiority. In such an unpleasant scene Breton was absolutely necessary.

But now. I reckon you get a finer class of surrealism, of weirdness-kick, in a story that has many traditional elements, with carefully written scene-settings and characterisations etc. The Strange is stronger if there's a Normal to compare it to. Yeah, I spend too long drafting and redrafting—Cyrano took 7 years in all; I was a twitchy machine overwound on anxiety; but I still believe that a classic novel is going to be one on which the author has worked very hard.

Dunno about the gradations of the surreal. The early drafts of Cyrano were written in a matter of fact style—'We entered a zoo wherein a Micro-organism House in the shape of a microscope rose above the grounds, containing within it bacteria the size of cows.' It evolved to become a series of slow, sly revelations—we follow Cyrano as he makes his discoveries—some attempts at suspense and 'realism' in order to make the weird all the more so…

I learned a little about illustration when doing drawings for the novel. I began by trying to be literal in my interpretations, but found that the drawings were uninteresting, and also that there was no need to be exact—the reader doesn't see the story, but conceives it—it occupies a conceptual space more than a visual one; like dreams (this is why movies and other art just can't do justice to dreams); the illustrations sort of reflected this—more allusive than literal. In that sense, they're more surreal than the text; but 'more abstract' is probably a better term

REP: Do *"Other Stories"* and *Other Stories* have a throughline? *Browne has a background in film and introduced me to this term years ago.* What ties the stories in your collection together?

AB: No, no throughline, in the sense that *The Silver Locusts* has one, say. But it's interesting to see them all gathered together; I remember reading collexions when I was a kid, and feeling steeped in that writer's sensibilities for the period of the read—a very definite sense of being in the author's head; I reckon there'll be some of the same sense should anyone read this; Jack Dann characterized the stories as 'winsome', which was spot-on—whimsy is another characteristic—a sort of post-innocent science-fiction whimsy?—Anna Tambour compared me to Edward Lear, which delighted me. So there's your answer: the throughline of the collexion involves qualities all beginning with 'W'.

REP: What was it like collaborating with John Dixon? Will you be collaborating with him again?

AB: John Dixon is the best. I think he had a hard childhood but man, his parents did something right. If a person lives long enough, more than likely a friend is going to die, and a friend is going to hit it big. Both have happened in my experience, in the first case so totally undeserving that it proves without question the dark indifference of the universe, in the second case, John's case, so deserving that it serves as proof of a benign god.

Anyway, yeah, he's supersmart and super-humble, so my neurotic fiddlings were tolerated and sometimes gentled aside. I loved the process. Our collective voice is quite different from our individual voices. It's like what I reckon happens during a Ouija Board session—you're communicating with the hive-mind come of the minds of everyone whose finger is on the planchette.

I dunno if a collab will happen again. I hope so. He's very busy, working very hard, and his sensibilities might have diverged a bit from weird sci fi—he's writing adventure/thriller stuff now, some horror. Not genres I like usually, but I recommend his books, which are intelligent and compassionate and fun.

REP: Is there anything you'd like to add?

AB: It's something I've been thinking about—dunno whether I agree with myself or not yet. It's about the benefits of writing. It's a narcisstic pursuit, like anything where you have to dig down deep into yourself—being an athlete, a high-order scientist, a soldier—but at least Narcissus could say he knew what he looked like. I've been thinking about Douglas Adams' quote about how he didn't know what he thought about something until he'd written a joke about it. The words I put on the page reflect myself back at me—through writing, I've come to know myself, or I think I have; the Delphic oracles would approve.

* * *

UPDATE: Adam Browne's *Tame Animals of Saturn* should be coming out later this year. "There'll be an orgiastic launch party and exhibition opening to mark the occasion," he says. Francis Greenslade and readers from Far Fetched Fables are recording an audio book of Browne's *"Other Stories" and Other Stories*. Andy Duncan, "the great animator and designer who made *The Adjustable Cosmos*, may turn one Dixon-Browne collaboration—*The Laughing Girl of Bora Fanong: A Tale of Colonial Venus*, originally published in *Andromeda Spaceways*—into a graphic novel. "We're going to be mounting a crowdfunding thing at some point," Browne says.

CBS cancelled *Intelligence*. The last episode aired March 31st. *Devil's Pocket*, the sequel to John Dixon's *Phoenix Island* is due out January 6, 2015.

The Steam Ornithopter

Story by Douglas Empringham
Illustration by Morland Gonsoulin

Rhing was midway along the alleyway when a puddle reflected a cat at his heels, keeping pace. Rather than a feral bruiser with scars and combat-notched ears, it was a tidy gray shorthair with green eyes. When it moved ahead of him and looked back, Rhing did the same. And there was a brown rat nearly equal the cat's size.

He drew his rapier as he spun on his heel and lunged. The rodent, not anticipating his move, was easily impaled. Rhing glancing about and seeing an open window above, flipped the rat through it.

On reaching Trader Street he crossed to the Restorative Bean, the coffeehouse where he was meeting Folie. The cat followed like a shadow. In the coffeehouse Rhing ordered and settled at a table near a stand of newspapers. He was browsing one when his stocky, ginger-haired friend strolled in and ordered a dish of coffee, generous on the cream.

Folie had scarcely seated himself when an urchin grimacing with pain appeared before him with a finger snared by a tiny trap.

"When they have eyes only for the prize," his friend said, "they become careless."

The trick coin, which when closed was identical to the silver florin being pushed toward Folie, opened like a clam when triggered then pinched shut. "A novelty made by an adept who calls them his 'sneak thief's bane.'"

"Jus' gets it off!" cried the boy.

"Listen young scholar of pick-pocketry, never forget you need all your fingers." Folie himself had been born into a family of thieves and coiners. For that reason, before working a release spell, he examined the boy's coin.

"Not amalgam but still false." He tossed it to Rhing.

It didn't have the telltale greasy feel of mercury. "What is it?"

"Plated lead glass."

When the cutpurse, in agony, grudgingly paid in honest silver, Folie removed the device. And caught the cat finishing his coffee. But his pique was gone in a flash. "Gray fur with green eyes is a handsome combination." He was that fond of cats.

As they strolled back to their inn, Rhing asked how matters stood with their caravan.

"All repairs made, the bedding laundered, and our team brushed and fed."

They entered their room at the Witch's Head to find the other two members of their troupe at (verbal) daggers drawn. As usual Jefery, a sometimes court fool about a yard tall, was getting the better of Lirec, a eunuch singer and juggler (and no giant at fifty-nine and a half inches).

"We need a holiday," Folie said.

"Where there are no nasty midges!" added Lirec.

Jefery, though, had been distracted by the cat standing behind Rhing. "No pets. Isn't that what we decided?"

"Does that include a talking cat," asked the cat, "enchanted by a sorcerer?"

"For the safety of all," Jefery insisted, "You must tell how you came to be enchanted."

"I agree," said Folie. "Must be cautious where sorcery is concerned."

The gray cat, without hesitation, sprang onto the bed and composed himself. "My name is Rommy. As a human young man I was popular with the damsels. Unlike my stepfather, who needs spells and gifts to carry out his adulteries. Then came a night when, in a fit of jealousy, he transformed me into a mouse before putting me in a crate with a hungry cat."

Folie cringed. "How truly I despise sorcerers…"

"The cat being hungry, it was the briefest of … *hunts.* " The cat shrank into a crouch. "The moment teeth threatened my tiny heart, I rebelled and thought *No!* I did not resort to weeping or special pleading. Just an emphatic *No!* And even as teeth stabbed into that terrified heart, I became this handsome gray tomcat."

"I have never heard of a plain denial staying the hand of Death, no matter how forcefully spoken," said Rhing. When he glanced at Folie, the other shook his head.

"I suppose the moment stays with you?" Jefery seemed more fascinated than horrified.

"Vividly. As to what Faust did with the mouse, I know not—for he tossed me out a window. Of a certainty my dreams would be nightmares if I had eaten that mouse…."

"A villain in spades!" said Folie.

"How did your stepfather discover the switch?" Rhing asked.

"I cannot guess. Faust's first rat assassin might have succeeded but for a lively old woman bashing its skull with her cane."

"I vote we let him use our portable haven," Folie said.

"Agreed," said Rhing. "He is safe from discovery while in there."

"What is this 'portable haven?' I am adverse to confined spaces."

Rhing brought the enchanted snuffbox from a hidden pocket in his coat. "You need not travel there if it is not agreeable." He next removed the shallow tray of ground tobacco. But as he adjusted the mirrored interior to catch the light, Lirec scooped up the cat.

"I shall be his guide and companion," said the eunuch, as they vanished.

Jefery kicked the space where Lirec had been standing. "And stay there!"

"We all could benefit from a vacation," Rhing said.

"Why not the mineral springs?" Folie asked "'We aren't but three days away."

No sooner had they agreed upon that than Jefery started to wonder if he might persuade Rommy to join him in a mock ventriloquist act.

* * *

The morning of the fourth day had them traveling on a road that canted upward onto a plateau renowned for its hot mineral springs, geysers and resorts. There was soon a billboard welcoming them and extolling the health benefits of their healing waters.

"When leisure starts to bore us, I suggest we perform Doctor Quack," said Jefery, who played the doctor's sly and jealous assistant.

"Their medical guild is famously strong," Folie said. "And physicians often have skins thinner than antique virgins."

"Time to recall our hidden companions," Rhing said.

Lirec and the cat came from the snuffbox stretching and yawning.

"I always knew," said the cat, "clouds would make fine pillows."

A second billboard promoted Vapora, Queen of Steam. Depicted was a handsome woman in a silky costume and wings. An image that startled the cat.

"Please don't see an evil omen in that," Lirec said.

"Not long before Faust turned on me," the cat said, "I overheard someone offer him a generous commission for maiming or killing Vapora. I would like nothing better than thwarting him, but … he is my enemy, not yours."

"And trying to balk a sorcerer is not my idea of a holiday," Folie insisted.

"Will he remember you in your present form?"

"I doubt it. His rat assassins were following my scent."

"It seems an ideal time for getting even," Jefery said. "He will be caught up in scheming and you are just another gray feline."

"If he worked a necromantic spell on the dead mouse," he might well know of your transmigration."

"I believe he'd do that," Rommy said, "wanting to gloat over my dying as a mouse."

"As I just said, you should be thirsting for revenge," Jefery put in.

"I have prayed and made burnt offerings to Nemesis many times," Rommy sighed. "I can only suppose there are many more deserving of retributive justice."

"On the chance he does know," Folie said, "I recommend your trusting to hair dye. It is not worth the risk or expense of using a glamour."

"Yes. Much as I like being a gray, black is a better disguise."

It was not long before the road crested and they entered a broken plain of cones and fissures issuing jets of steam. Not long after they arrived at the village of Vulcan's Heart. Travel beyond this point was by steam-driven trolley.

They chose the least expensive appearing inn, and the supper portions were indeed modest, but the bill was extravagant. In addition they learned that no new permits were being issued to players or other entertainers. And Folie's comment also proved true: to protect the mineral spring resorts and local practitioners, physicians, barber-surgeons, tooth-pullers, bone-setters and herbalists from elsewhere were forbidden to practice.

"We said we deserved a holiday," Rhing said, "and Fate has closed all other doors."

Fortunately Lirec heard from a servitor (a fellow eunuch) of an elderly couple that let wagons park on their properly for a modest consideration. This took them to a yard surrounded by low brick buildings, some partially underground. But while the fee for parking in the yard was low, the purchase of water and fodder for their horses was equally high.

While the four visited a resort, Rommy would stay with the caravan. At his disposal was a toothy guard dog conjured by Folie, one that would obey no one but the cat.

"Having dominion over a vicious dog," Jefery said: "must be every cat's dream."

* * *

The following day was equally cloudless, as little rain fell between early spring and late autumn. The steam-driven trolley to the geyser huffed noisily but was otherwise comfortable. Though open at the sides, there was a wide metal awning to shelter riders.

The resort they chose was Vitality Wells, and there they soaked in the springs, received massages, and drank cups of the healing waters. It was a refreshing (albeit expensive) excursion.

Rommy was equally well rested, having had no occasion to raise their guard dog.

* * *

The next day Lirec stayed with the caravan. He wanted to replace strings on his lute and harp plus work on song ideas.

When they boarded the steam-trolley, the cat was dyed black and the others wore sunhats. The amphitheater they were delivered to was on a hillside and overlooking the geyser. The more expensive seats were on upper tiers and under a roof. The cat chose to watch for his stepfather from this shady place.

Rhing and the others took unreserved seats in the lower rows, cheaper due to their being in the sun—and a slight risk of being splashed by scalding water. To protect them Folie cast a shield spell.

As the expected time of the geyser's eruption approached, a crew working hand cranks extended a wide gangplank till the disk at the end nearly touched the geyser's cone. Then Vapora appeared in a red helmet, gauntlets and one-piece costume. But she did not step onto the steel plank and walk to the disk until her crew had buckled on folded wings and adjusted a frame with the gearing that permitted her to flex the wings.

"I am the One and Only *Vapora!*" she cried, in a carrying voice. Her silky costume, she explained, was fashioned from chrysotile fibers more fireproof than asbestos.

"I am a daredevil," she added, expansively, "not a reckless idiot!"

The crowd greeted this with applause.

"I like her already," Jefery said. He despised false modesty.

"Mine is a feat of skill and mechanics," she went on, striding boldly out the gangplank. "There is no magic involved, not even protective spells. But of course you are free to look to your own safety."

Rommy joined them, keeping to their shadows. The cat had been unable to locate Grandmaster Faust, but he had seen a vendor selling fancy masks with eyepieces charmed to penetrate glamours.

When Folie heard the man described, he said, "Delan! I know him! And a pair of his eyeglasses are just what we need." He then hurried away.

"I should have foreseen that Faust would employ a glamour!" moaned the cat.

Vapora, now balanced in the center of the disk, expanded her wings to a cocked position.

"Flawless poise and panache," Jefery chirped. "A headliner, and doesn't she know it."

Rhing's interest had shifted to the wings.

Folie came back to report that Faust had threatened Delan into letting him alter his lenses so none exposed him. But the artisan had withheld a monocle, which he'd lent to Folie. "For all Delan is mortally afraid of the sorcerer, but wants no part in harming Vapora."

A garishly dressed youth (who resembled Vapora) now came marching slowly down the steps while tapping on a snare drum and heralding the geyser impending upsurge. He reached the bottom step a moment before the geyser erupted, thrusting Vapora upward. And when the spout of boiling water and steam reached its zenith, with a shout she extended her wings fully and glided free.

"Doesn't she dance a gloriously fine line between daring and lunacy!" Jefery laughed, standing on his seat to applaud.

Vapora, pedaled to flap her wings while directing her flight toward vents then riding their jets of steam. Thus she soared like a bird riding updrafts, while an unseen calliope played a rousing tune, likewise using captured steam.

Folie was holding the monocle to the cat's eye when he picked out his stepfather among the crew. "Faust is among the roustabouts—and doing as little work as possible."

Vapora now wheeled back to end her performance by sailing over the audience, trimming and gathering her wings, then dropping gracefully into a net. Greeted by the enthusiastic praise and applause few performers ever hear.

When Folie gave Rhing the monocle, he saw that beneath the glamour of a weathered and sinewy roustabout was a thickset, warty toad of a man.

Vapora's crew unstrapped her wings while her daughter brought a towel and a refreshing cup. Then her helmet was removed and her admirers were permitted to surround her.

Faust did naught but remain in the background. The cat went nearer, from shadow to shadow, hoping to hear the person who'd hired the sorcerer.

"Thankfully he seems a cautious knave, waiting for an ideal opportunity," Folie said, as they went for iced drinks.

Rommy did not return from eavesdropping until they were walking to the trolley. And he was agitated. After springing into Folie's arms, he whispered: "Complication! The person I heard commissioning my stepfather is ... *Vapora herself!*"

No one spoke until they were seated on the last bench in steam-trolley's last car.

"I overheard," Folie said, "that whenever she isn't able, her daughter does the act."

"She is also teaching her son," Jefery added. "He was that drummer boy."

"Family infighting can get treacherous," Rhing said. His father was a baron and his mother a king's cousin.

"I vote we don't interfere," said Folie.

"But you could still aid me," the cat said, "in getting even."

"What better time to sandbag Faust," said the midget, "than when he's caught up in earning his hire?"

"Said the pride 'n joy of the gallows bird family," moaned Folie, to the midget's delight.

"Let Rommy first consider the consequences of failure," Rhing said.

"Master adepts are seldom as jolly and forbearing as nursernaids," Folie said, wryly.

"Neat bit of understatement," Rhing said, laughing and patting his friend on the back.

"Now ... *now* I am having second thoughts," admitted Rommy.

Having neglected to whisper, he instantly attracted the notice of two small children who were delighted by the prospect of a talking cat. But Jefery, quick as ever, impersonated Romrny's voice and Folie juggled a cascade. The children were disappointed but their parents were content to dismiss them as mere players.

* * *

On their return, Folie and Lirec practiced their juggling routines while Jefery and Rhing considered some new stage business to freshen their plays.

After their supper, Folie and Rhing went to feed the horses and, now that sun was waning, turn them out in the paddock. They had no sooner done so, closed the gate, and lit their pipes when an older bearded man, wide and swarthy, came from scrub at the paddock's far side. As he tried to climb over the railing he slipped, fell against it, and clung. A hand stained red came from under his cloak as he reached out.

"Farold ... help me...!" With rattling groan he then collapsed in a heap.

"Gowan!" cried Folie, whose name was Farold. "You wretch! Abandoned me without a coin or a crust and now you seek my aid? The gods ought to set a limit on gall!"

"No need to ask if this is one of your former masters."

"That sink of dross must have seen me watching Vapora." As Rhing swung over the railing and started across the paddock, Folie added, "Do not offer help on my account."

"I suspect he's beyond that."

The man's stillness and blank stare proved him correct. When he saw the bloody slash in his robe, he knew the cause. "Now, where's his horse or mule...?"

A moment after he'd climbed atop the fence he saw a saddled horse sprawled and lifeless amidst the scrub and cacti. Once nearer the beast he could soon tell Folie, "By the lather, its eyes, and its lolling tongue, I'd say your Master Gowan rode his mount to death."

"Just the heartless sort to do that. A terrible master." As he swung over the fence and came to join him, Folie added: "Leave his saddlebags to me, they're sure to be warded."

Rommy arrived while Folie was probing the horse and its tack for defenses.

"Faust never brought that dead man to the house," the cat said. "Not while I was there."

When Folie opened the near saddlebag, out tumbled a narrow volume bound in black leather. It had neither title nor author but was embossed with a red viper's head.

"Faust's grimoire!" cried the cat. "And sure to be warded."

"If it was, Gowan overcame it," Folie said, after conjuring a detection spell. "All I find is a simple guardian spell easily gotten around."

"It contains powerful sorcery, if he filched it from my stepfather," said the cat, crouching and glancing about nervously, "that's what brought death to him."

They were crossing to the gate when Rhing looked up and sighted the largest vulture he had ever seen. Which, upon reaching the dead horse, immediately set about tearing through the saddlebags with beak and talons.

The cat fled. While they distanced themselves, Folie urged him to open the snuffbox.

And the grimoire had no sooner vanished into that enchanted dimension then the carrion bird flew from horse to rider. It was only then, seeing it closer, that he realized it was carved and painted wood.

"That monster Faust transformed a ship's figurehead!"

"Further proof that Gowan was an utter fool to steal from him!"

The carrion bird, not finding what it sought, rose in the air. But after hovering a moment it dropped back, tore open Gowan's chest, and plucked out his heart.

"It's turning back means someone is scrying us!" Folie said. "Pray they aren't using a crystal or mirror large enough to show fine detail…!"

When the articulated figurehead again sought to take flight, a flash of blue spell-energy enfolded and consumed it, leaving only charred and smoldering fragments that panicked the horses and mules.

Rhing and Folie were calming their horses when they heard the drumming of many more.

And around the corner of the stable came ten men in armor led by a duke known to Rhing and a young master adept recognized by Folie.

"Did he speak to you?" demanded the wiry and snappish adept, pointing at Gowan.

"Only to beg aid," answered Folie. "He died before saying more."

"But it was to his horse that the creature went first, your grace," Rhing told the ruddy bearded duke, indicating where the animal had fallen.

"All we saw it take was the man's heart," Foilie added.

"If my magic did not destroy the book along with the creature," the adept said, as he searched Gowan, "his rogue found a place to hide it."

"Can that devil Faust root it out?" asked the duke.

"He will or die trying, sir. He lives by it, for his memory has become faulty."

When the young adept failed to detect the grimoire anywhere near, they were dismissed. Once around the corner of the stable, Folie said:

"I would as soon be rid of that book."

"I cannot suggest we surrender it, for my brother told me of the duke recently taking a young *and very ambitious wife.*"

"Now there is a fine reason to keep it well hid!" Folie admitted.

* * *

No more came of the ducal visit. They packed and were gone not long after first light.

Rhing drove with Jefery and Lirec on either side. Rommy was inside the caravan browsing the

grimoire with a reluctant yet curious Folie. But in the end they found nothing able to reverse the cat's enchantment.

It was Lirec, as the road made a right angle bend, who caught sight of Vapora in flight. Though she was away from steam vents,

"What is keeping her up?" he leaned inside and asked Folie.

"She isn't pedaling to work the wings … She's struggling to alter direction and close the wings. Which means she is in the grip of someone's spell-working."

When they came to a side road and Vapora slanted in that direction, Rhing reined the horses to follow.

"It's definitely magic that's keeping her up," Folie said, leaning past Lirec to watch.

"A carriage has turned," said the cat, looking back, "and will soon overtake us. The two in front wear masks, and there's a third riding on the rear footboard."

The road went around a shoulder of the hill and ended at a closed gate. At their approach an old man came running from the shade of a tree to place himself in front of the gate. With his rude staff he pointed to a sign that read: PAINTED ROCKS GORGE IS CLOSED TO ALL BUT THOSE WITH A WRITTEN PASS FROM THE DUKE.

"Painted rocks are petrified wood!" Lirec said. "I've seen pictures."

"No samples, no souvenirs!" cried the gatekeeper. "That's unlawful!"

By standing on the driving bench Rhing could view one end a winding gorge. "It looks like a huge fractured geode."

Folie was doing his magical utmost to help Vapora fly clear of the gorge. And only now did the gatekeeper see the flier. Bracing himself against the gate, he waved his staff and wailed: "How do I keep m'darlin' rocks safe from likes a that?"

Folie's efforts were helping Vapora stay airborne. But then the carriage arrived and the passenger wearing a red leather mask hurled a bolt of blue spell-energy that stunned Folie and put him on his back.

The curious thing that Rhing noted was that Faust appeared to be taking orders from the carriage driver, who wore a flesh-colored veil.

The flier, instead of soaring, was being pulled back over the gorge, despite her defiant acrobatic exertions. The attack on Folie sent Lirec and Jefery diving for cover inside the caravan. It also caused the gatekeeper to flee up the hillside.

Then Rhing felt his belt knife jerked from its sheaths. It joined those of the others at the sorcerer's feet, where they twisted and were melted together. But none of his other weapons came from inside the caravan, to his relief.

Faust's mask gave way to a new glamour. This new illusion presented a handsome and virile man not yet thirty. And the glint in his dark eyes left little doubt that he was pondering other mischief. Rhing had seldom felt so helpless.

Then, however, the driver jumped down and ordered, "To business! You said only that one had magic."

Vapora! The same voice Rhing had heard at the geyser.

The sorcerer, though his jaw worked mutinously, nodded. As he went striding toward the gate, it burst open and disintegrated.

"You!" Vapora said, tapping Rhing's arm. "you look strong enough to help."

He replied with a slight bow and a wry smile. "The honor overwhelms me."

"A roustabout is needed, not a courier," said Vapora, laughing behind her veil.

Looking back, Rhing saw Lirec and Jefery help a dazed Folie stand on rubbery legs. And together they managed to lift and shove him inside the caravan.

When Vapora whistled, the youth who'd been riding on the carriage tailboard, came running. He was fourteen or fifteen and had her brunet coloring and oval face.

"No drum today?" Rhing asked. He recognized the boy from Vapora's act.

"Sees you don't make jokes on Fausty," the other whispered.

"I've seen his work elsewhere. A sorcerer tried and true."

"I'm a flier an' a mechanic, too, not jus'a drummer."

As they came to the edge of the gorge, a gust of natural wind appeared to be lifting the flier clear of the painted rocks. Then Faust, with a nasty laugh, gestured and spoke words of power and she stalled, wobbled, and plunged headfirst into the cliff below them. They heard rather than saw her collision with the rock wall.

"The ungrateful mutineer wanted to take my act to new heights," Vapora bit off each word cleanly, without a hint of sentiment. "She got her wish. I hope she is content."

Removing her veil, she told Rhing: "You will help Canute recover the wings and costume. My son knows what to do. And you will be paid for your trouble."

Rhing nodded. If he refused, she was sure to sic Faust on him.

Canute had brought a coil of line, one end of which he secured to a scrub oak. It wasn't a difficult descent as hand- and footholds were plentiful, if sharp-edged. And there was little in the way of loose scree at the bottom. That, he surmised, had long since been carried off as souvenirs or for jewelry.

Canute's dead sister was kneeling against the scarp, held up by her wings. Her flying costume was little damaged and she had protected her face by holding up her arms defensively.

The youth was frankly relieved. He'd worried that in sliding down the rocky scarp she'd been, "Grated like a cheese."

Rhing supported the wings while Canute released the harness straps and folded back the pedals. Vapora had warned them to be patient and gentle with her wings. And having been fully spread they had suffered only slight abrasions and the loss of a few feathers. He could see no irreparable damage.

"Step away from the cliff and hold the wings up," Faust instructed.

When Rhing obeyed, a spell carried them up to an anxious Vapora. Once she had them, the sorcerer warned that he was preparing a cremation spell.

But Vapora overruled him. "I want the flying suit—I told you that not twenty minutes ago!"

"Blood stains, rips and all?"

"It is still valuable to me!" She then gave Rhing the chore of removing the suit.

He had wondered what the flier wore underneath. What he discovered was a sleeveless, one-piece black silk garment covering a leanly muscled, small breasted, and slim-hipped figure. The body of her mother before she was born, Rhing thought.

The suit, helmet and boots went up by rope. While they waited for it to be sent back, Canute whispered, "These pretty rocks sell for sweet prices."

"I doubt you risk much by taking a few pieces, your mother *is* an institution."

The rope dropped back but they waited until after Faust worked his fire spell. The cremation was over in a moment and not attended by the stench of burning flesh.

Canute now slid a small folded canvas sack

from under his tunic. What made him even bolder was the sound of heated words passing between Vapora and the sorcerer.

"They're not thinking 'bout us," the boy whispered.

While Canute harvested loose, mineral-colored rocks, Rhing looked about. The colors reminded him of those used in illuminated manuscripts, Temptation came on apace, and he did not resist. Encouraged by the dispute above.

Faust had hold of the wings and was envisioning himself flying. "I shall be Vapora! With a few artful and subtle spells I shall improve the act."

"Listen to me this time! The soul of *my* act is acrobatic *skill!* Cheapen it with magic and you shall be caught out! Or do you imagine yourself the only powerful adept?"

"I admit I am not alone at the top. But so many of the others have scruples by the scruple, conscience by the dram and a few grains of honor."

"All you will succeed in doing it getting my act discredited!"

"Magic frees me to do as I please, that's why I made it my study."

Rhing climbed around Canute. At the top he saw Vapora and Faust face to face. He also saw the cat under the caravan, watching intently from between the spokes of a wheel. And Lirec and Jefery peering from inside the caravan.

"You fulfilled our bargain and there is your gold!"

Faust did not even glance at the full purse she brought from beneath her duster.

"I took the commission out of curiosity. It offered something new and novel."

Canute left off harvesting and tucked himself into a shallow cave. Rhing stayed where he was with a firm grasp on the rope, watching as Faust, holding the wings up, trotted about and hummed merrily. As he went by, Vapora pulled a dagger from her sleeve and stabbed his back.

Or tried to. The sorcerer, ready for just that, hopped out of harm's way. "I was certain you could be provoked! This is the treat I prepared for when you did!"

Faust smirked and giggled as he conjured. And Vapora was gripped by a precipitous aging and wasting. She barely had time to groan before she was bent and crooked, decrepit and wheezing, her eyes rheumy, her hair thin and white. When her strength and balance failed and she collapsed to her knees,

Faust mocked her sudden helplessness by dancing around her and giving her playful kicks.

Gasping curses through her agony and anger, Vapora set about crawling laboriously toward the edge of the gorge.

"Cowardice? No no! You have never appreciated who I am or what powers I command. Now listen, hag, Grandmaster Faust does not accept cowardice!" He then put himself in her path and cast anew. Too late he awoke to eight pounds of gray-dyed-black cat hurtling toward him from under the caravan. He was only left time to squeal before he was punched in the belly by a fist that nimbly sprang clear.

Over the edge the sorcerer went, flailing rather than spell-weaving. Unable rise above incredulity and outrage before an edge of mineral-dyed rock split his skull like a ripe melon.

It took Vapora several minutes to recover her younger self. After a cleansing laugh she told Canute to plunder the dead grandmaster.

But Rhing caught the boy by the sleeve. "Faust is just the sort of adept to arm himself with a hex or curse, should he die suddenly."

And Folie leaned from the caravan to readily and graphically tell her what curses and hexes a sorcerer might affect, even when dead.

"Be content to save yourself the price of his hire," Jefery put in.

"All things considered," Vapora said, with a shudder, "I think that most excellent advice." And her son agreed. But the two stayed to share a glass of brandy.

She asked if they intended to camp there. Rhing said it was too risky. "We could be blamed for the ruined gate. And even accused of causing Faust's death."

Presently they followed the carriage to the main road where they parted, each group going its separate way. But as they drove, Folie and Rommy cheerfully announced that Faust's grimoire held a spell that nullified booby traps.

"We may plunder the ole sorcerer with impunity!" Folie said, thrilled at the prospect.

After waiting off road while they ate a light meal, Rhing turned the caravan around and drove back. They looked for the gatekeeper at Painted Rocks without finding him, which was welcome news.

"But we must not tarry," he said. "Surely he has gone to report."

Lirec and he climbed down while Folie and Jefery kept watch and the cat paced along the cliff edge, Grandmaster Faust rewarded them with several purses in addition to rings, bracelets, silver buckles and jeweled clasps.

Rhing having told them of having taken some already, they climbed up without stopping for petrified wood. And kept the excellent rope.

Rommy greeted them with: "Now that the gallows bird has been picked clean, I should like to give him a full taste of his own cremation spell."

"A tasty morsel of poetic justice!" the midget laughed.

Folie retrieved the spell-book and conjured while Lirec held Rommy so he could witness the burning. When it was over, the cat said:

"Obliterating Faust was extravagantly satisfying."

"One less sorcerer causing misery and mischief," a smiling Folie added.

"It also tidies up nicely," Rhing laughed. "We shall be gone without a trace."

"No fear of being haunted?" Lirec asked the cat, as they drove away.

"A trifle. Especially if his book leads me to the fabled nine lives."

"You are purring," Jefery observed.

"Effortlessly," replied the cat. "A sensation that is even nicer on the inside."

Goose Witches

Deep inside a cave hidden inside a mountain
An ancient church keeps genealogical records
with massive stacks of paper piled
over ten thousand pages high.
There are rows and rows of stacks of paper
stretching back deep into the cavern for who knows how far.
As one descends deeper and deeper into the cavern
the further you go the more gnome-like the record keepers become,
stunted and twisted,
their light sources dimmer and dimmer.
One woman told me she had researched her family tree
and discovered that one of her ancestors
was a bona fide witch.
She even had a wand
but it seems that her magical powers
were limited to the acquisition of other people's geese.
This witch would wave her wand
and geese would flock to her.
It sounds innocent enough but among the Apache people
goose magic was associated with the ability to acquire ammunition.
It makes me wonder if this wand waving sorceress
wasn't planning to gather her fowl army in an attempt at conquest and empire.
At least these were the thoughts I was thinking
on a chilly cold cloudy evening
when suddenly I heard overhead
the honking of a migrating flock of geese.
Was it really migration or was it troop movements
Because for just a moment the clouds parted
and I could have sworn I had seen
the lead geese in the front of the V
with a rider astride
in bonnet and petticoats.

— Gary Every

Pattern Sense

Story by F.T. McKinstry
Illustration by Kathy Ferrell

It all started with a mouse.

Persistent creatures, mice, driven as all things are by the turn of winter's gaze, but with the added cunning of the nocturnal. In early autumn, they found a crack in the eaves of Melisande's cottage on the wooded outskirts of Ull. The swordsman had repaired the crack before returning to the towers and yards of Osprey on Sea, the great hall over the snow-draped Thorgrim Mountains, where he served. What a swordsman knew of carpentry, well, that was open to question. But he knew other things. Nice things.

As the moon waxed, the mice kept Melisande up at night, their tiny feet pattering in the rafters, claws scraping, teeth gnawing. How such a small creature could make such a racket eluded her almost as much as her lover's carpentry skills. The cat, being wise in the ways of the season, knew all, for he did not sleep at night, not when the moon was bright and certainly not when leaves spiraled down to carpet the frosty earth. No, he hunted. But the mice knew that.

It was the eve of the Hunter's Moon when Melisande first noticed something odd in her latest knitting project, a thick winter tunic for the young goatherd who lived at the bottom of the hill. The wool, deep brown as the smoke-stained rafters of the cottage ceiling, formed gaps where the sleeve joined the yoke, much like the cracks between a wall and a roof. Deep in her mind, the observation awoke a visceral awareness of interconnection, the wisdom of the natural world, a tapestry of patterns, lines, curves and counts as perfectly cast as a well-stitched swatch.

Pattern sense, her mother once called it; at least Melisande thought it might have been her, though it could have been her grandmother, or one of the old women in the village. Come to think of it, her mother had turned a dark eye on such things. Being of a wilder mind, Melisande picked up her needles, hummed softly and wove a neat kitchener stitch over the gaps in the armpit of her work.

She did not hear the mice that night, the night after, or the night after that. Melisande wondered if the cat's vigilance had finally paid off. Clever hunters, cats. So she told herself as her pattern sense curled quietly as a snake in an ivy patch, to rest with both eyes open.

* * *

The swordsman did not return to Melisande that winter, though she plucked and snipped the white woolen threads of a blanket's edge to keep the snow from the woodland path to her cottage. When the snows melted and she had folded her woolens and hung her snowshoes behind the door, still, he did not come. Accompanied by her old gray knitting bag, she wandered the streets of Ull and the sheep-dappled foothills of Thorgrim listening for rumors of war, but heard none. When the air became hot, she knit brindled patterns of drops and sky to soak the earth with rain. She knit green leaves and pulled threads of weeds from the vegetable patch, leaving purple violets here and there to grace the air with her lover's favorite scent. But he did not return, as he had each moon for two suns past.

Perhaps he had found another sweetheart. A younger woman unstained by time and pattern sense. Why would he stay with a votary of needles and wool? Men such as he did not take wives or stay with lovers. They roamed like tomcats.

Still, she waited.

On the first day of summer, Melisande rose early, put on water for tea, fed the cat and went outside into the fog that cloaked the forest. A goat bleated in the mist. The village carpenter, in return for blankets for his children, now protected from cold and smiling in their dreams, had built her a shelter surrounded by a sturdy fence. It was now home to a nanny that the goatherd gave Melisande in return for his tunic, a very fine tunic, he said, that banished the rain from his bones.

After feeding the goat, Melisande fetched her tea and her knitting bag and walked to the stone bench on the edge of her garden, thickening with seedlings the village women had given her in return for tea cozies, placemats and shawls. Nary a puff of steam, drop of ale or chilling draft eluded her stitches, they claimed.

She drew forth the folds of a cloak for the constable's daughter. Pale green as fresh grass, it had an intricate symmetrical pattern of wine-red climbing roses with dark green leaves. The shepherd's wife, in return for a dress of silken flax, dyed and spun the knitter's yarn in lovely colors of summer fields. Melisande drew a deep breath as she gathered up her needles and spread the soft, fine wool across her lap....

Her mind went blank.

In the center of the back, in a red rose tinged with pink and shimmering with dew, was a ragged hole. Blinking, she pulled it up and touched the popped loops of several missing stiches. She muttered an ugly word fit for swordsmen over drink. When was the last time she had dropped a stitch?

She jumped as something clattered on the other side of the cottage. Hoofbeats. Her arm hit the teacup by her side, knocking it off the bench with a clink and a splash. Between the trees beyond the path, a rider came into view. Melisande's heart turned a triple beat as he dismounted.

Leaving her knitting by the garden, she ran to the swordsman, ignoring the sadness on his broad shoulders and the way his hand slid reluctantly from the reins of his dark charger. She flung her arms around him like a girl. He returned her embrace but weakly. Chilled, she withdrew. Age touched his long dark hair and the stubble on his face. His gray eyes held something she had not seen before, a blurred focus like that of a seedpod closing to an early frost.

"Othin," she greeted him. She had never felt the name, taken from a god of wisdom, trickery and war, much suited him. Now, it seemed to. Her joy soaked into the ground like spilled tea.

"Melisande," he returned, avoiding any affectionate nickname or other.

Details became clear and distant at the same time. He did not retrieve a bag from his saddle. Instead of the gentle garb of a man come to rest in the company of his woman, he wore the trappings of his station: shining mail, polished leather and glinting steel. Melisande stepped back, engulfed by a storm tide of self-conscious alarm. White threads in her hair, thin cracks on the corners of her eyes, she had become a priestess of pattern sense, a cruel goddess of time gone by, icy fingers of midwinter nights and a careless hole in the rose-red heart of her finest work.

"Do you go to war?" she asked, knowing it was not so.

The swordsman lowered his gaze briefly, as if to gather resolve from a void untouched by need. "I have taken a wife."

Melisande stepped back again, catching her foot on a stone as the blood left her cheeks. Her heart started to pound. "Why return only to tell me this?" A reasonable question.

"I wanted you to know. I am sorry."

He turned from her with controlled urgency, mounted his steed and rode away into the morning mist without looking back.

* * *

Melisande turned around on the path like the first purl row on a long scarf. Birds chirruped in the trees. The goat bleated.

A wife. Was it better to know the fate of a cat gone missing than to be left hoping for and imagining something kinder than the truth? She moved unsteadily to the garden bench where the maiden's cloak lay half draped on the ground beside the broken teacup. A chill crept up her spine as she bent to retrieve it.

A dropped stitch in the heart of a rose. Surely not.

The cloak slipped from her fingers. Flooding into the wake of her scorned heart came a ferocious, ice-jammed torrent of what was and what might have been; the swordsman's touch, his smile, the sound he made in his throat when rolling her into bed, the clumsy way he had muscled a ladder to the wall to fix a crack. Dark spots filled her eyes as she walked to the cottage. What use had she for marriage? For her work, the villagers helped her. And children? Pah! She preferred cats. A goat. A garden with violets.

For all that, a swordsman was quite nice to care for.

She reached the door in a near run as the pain flooded down. She had never asked the war god to be true to her; she preferred him free. What did she expect?

A *wife?*

She entered the cottage and stumbled to her knitting cabinet. She flung open the doors, ripped the drawers from their tracks and rifled through yarn until she found a skein of blood red. Tears streaming down her face, she clutched the coils in her fist like a beating heart, snatched up a pair of elegant needles and sank to her knees, pattern sense rising and falling in her fingers like the breath of a dragon. She could change this. End this. Turn of a heart, death of a wife, fall of a trickster. She could—

With a cry, she dropped her woolen heart and threw the needles skittering across the floor. Then she buried her face in her tingling hands and wept.

* * *

Melisande eventually finished the constable's daughter's cloak. Quietly as an old grave, she had picked up and wove in the dropped stitches with no intention to alter her swordsman's heart from its cruel course, as she might have done.

Instead, she knit pattern sense into tears and let them fall.

The villagers had never known rain and cold as they did that summer. Within a charger's ride of Melisande's cottage, the rivers overran their banks, forests hung low, crops drowned in their rows and sheep grazed in mud. Mushrooms and slugs took up residence on garden paths and in the shadows of rotting fruit. Finally, at the urging of the goatherd, those in the know gathered and headed for the knitter's cottage.

Melisande looked up from her work at a knock on the door. "Millie," called a familiar voice. She moved from under the voluminous folds of a dark gray blanket thick with black threads, and went to answer for her stitches.

A small group of men and women stood in the rain wearing Melisande's fine work: the miller a sweater, the thatcher a vest, the goatherd his tunic and the constable's daughter her cloak. Clutching a woolen cap to his chest, the carpenter flicked a nervous glance at the steely sky. "Millie, lass. Will you not help us?" His large brown eyes grew gentle, almost desperate.

No one had ever called Melisande a witch, a dusty term used more often in cities than in the wilds, where folk lived with things like pattern sense even if they did not possess the skill to wield it. But the villagers' presence here wrought truth from suspicion.

"'Tis your own business," said the midwife. "But if I didn't know no better, I'd say your heart's been broken."

The others mumbled and nodded, shifting on their feet. The blacksmith, whom the swordsman used to visit during his stays in the valley, glanced up with telling brevity.

Melisande lowered her gaze to the ground, her fingers tingling with the dragon's breath. It was labored, now, not as bright and lithe as it once had been.

"We're your kith and kin," said the goatherd.

The simple statement scattered Melisande's thoughts like finding a mouse nest in a yarn drawer. Since the swordsman had abandoned her to the subtle whispers of pattern sense, kith and kin had become a cat, a goat and a garden patch. But these were her people. As they waited, their faces filled with love and sadness, she understood. Pattern sense was not a thing of mortals. Its roots had no bottom, no end, no definition; it lay in her hands to give it form. She looked up, gulped back tears with a grateful nod, and returned inside.

She spent all that night unraveling the black from the gray, twisting it into silent skeins and putting it away. Then she pulled out blue and gold, and began to cast stitches.

The next morning, sunlight dawned upon the soaked, glittering land.

* * *

By summer's end, news of war reached the valley.

Melisande hid her feelings beneath a comfortable cloak of group concern. But war has the ears of wolves, and the Lords of Osprey on Sea soon heard of a knitter in the village of Ull with a remarkably deft hand. One dreary day, two soldiers arrived on fine mounts, knocked on Melisande's door and respectfully commissioned her to make clothing to warm the king's army in the coming months. She bowed her head, holding a hand over her heart to hide the scar.

With somber industry, the soldiers provided her with yarn in shades of forests in winter. As the shadows grew long and the days shorter, Melisande worked, her pattern sense quiescent but aware, touching her hands like moonlight breaking through swiftly moving clouds. Neat stacks of socks, gloves, sweaters, leggings, and blankets filled the corners of her cottage until the soldiers came to carry them off in carts filled with the villagers' offerings—including young men fit for battle. Three times they came, their horses thumping up the path, breaking Melisande from the needles' rhythm. Three times she provided them with wares, her fingers rough and sore and her heart knowing the fear of every wife and maid with a swordsman's favor.

Until one day.

The trees had lost their leaves a full moon past. The garden had been harvested and stored in the root cellar. Wind whispered in the chimney top, drawing drafts mingled with the smell of two-day-old soup warming on the stove. Melisande worked a blanket of white and considered another long winter without the warmth of a man in her bed. Without thinking, she eyed a skein of sun-gold yarn tucked into a shelf in the open wool cabinet.

Hoofbeats startled her from the blur of a long-lost notion. Her fingers tingled as she looked up at the window, pale twilight fading from the sky. It had not been long since the soldiers last came and she had only a few things to give them.

After an odd time, a heavy hand fell upon the door.

Her throat dry, Melisande rose to answer it. A blast of cold air whirled snowflakes into her face.

"Millie?" the dark figure said, pushing back his hood.

A shock of blood raced in her veins. She had almost imagined this while recently casting an extra stitch onto a row with an odd count.

"May I come in?" Othin asked. She nodded and moved out of the way. The swordsman entered, closed the door and hung his cloak on the hook as if he had lived there all his life. His cheeks were wind-burned and his warrior's trappings were dulled by trouble. His raven hair was bound on his back with a piece of blue yarn. "I took the liberty of caring for my horse. I found feed in the loft."

Still speechless, Melisande nodded. The village groom, who quite loved the barley-brown scarf she had knit for him, had put feed in her lean-to stable for the soldiers' horses. She gestured to the low stack of woolens in the corner, some of it unfinished. "I don't have much done if that's why you're here." A daft comment. "But there's soup if you're hungry."

"I am that." He pulled out a chair at the table and sat. She shuffled to the stove feeling as old and unkempt as her tattered gray knitting bag. "I didn't come for woolens," he added behind her.

Melisande stirred the soup. Truly, she had knit the dropped stitches in the constable's daughter's cloak with nothing but tears, her pattern sense buried in the earth like an onion plug. If she had known the swordsman would return, she would have buried it deeper.

"Millie," he said quietly to the silence. "Forgive me."

She set a bowl and spoon before him, and then a half-loaf of hard bread covered by a soft-knit cloth with black cats stitched in it. "I never asked you to stay," she reminded him. All knitting had closure in a bound-off row. Had she not taken great care to close every seam, gusset and neckband to protect the soldiers from cold and harm? Pattern sense favored such things.

The swordsman stared into his soup. "She is the captain's daughter," he began. The cold draft on Melisande's heart told her to whom he referred. "She told him I had gotten her with child." He picked up the spoon and lifted a dripping bite to his mouth. "I never touched her. But had I not taken her to wife I'd have been released from my station to a life of dishonor."

Melisande sat down and put her hands in her lap. The trouble with binding off too tightly, she mused, was that the ribbing would not give. Twice, her fingers tingling, she had unraveled the stitches above the bind to end it differently.

The swordsman continued: "When news arrived that armies from across the sea planned to plunder our shores on the eve of winter, our minds turned to provisions. A man in my company had a fine cloak he claimed to have bought in Ull." He looked up, his gray gaze touching her softly. "I'd have known those stitches anywhere."

The blacksmith. He had traded the cloak Melisande made him to a soldier in return for more time to make swords. She had run out of black wool and used the soldiers' gray along the trim, thinking it outstanding.

"On my wedding day," Othin said, tearing off a chunk of bread, "I decided I would leave her and take to the road as a mercenary. My feelings must have shown in my response to the cloak. She branded me a blackguard and cast me from the house."

Melisande had had one less sock after pilfering the soldiers' yarn to finish the blacksmith's cloak. Humming, she had settled for a mismatched pair. They would be hidden inside of boots. Well, most of the time.

"You don't look like a mercenary," she observed.

He set his spoon into the bowl. "I'm not. When she did not grow with child, her father forced the truth from her. She intended to snare me after the wedding and hope no one took note of the days."

Melisande rose to take the swordsman's bowl. On their second visit, the soldiers had asked, while nervously looking around at anything but her, if she might knit a pocket in the crotches of their leggings that they might take care of their business more easily. She did apologize for not having thought of that.

"I got lucky," Othin said with a dry smile, for he did not believe in luck. He rose, moved to the fire and placed a piece of birch on the flames. "Your wood pile is sound." He looked over his shoulder. "Did the mice return?"

Ignoring the question, Melisande went to his side. "Why have you come here, Othin?"

The name had never fit him so well as now, as he knelt there gazing with seasoned wisdom into the fire. He said, "The old men claimed never to have seen the likes of the storm that came. 'Tis now believed the raiders' entire fleet went down."

"Then there'll be no war?"

He shrugged. "Nothing we can't handle, if anything."

On the last new moon, it had occurred to Melisande, while deftly casting on the stitches of a sailor's cap, that storms at sea could be terrible this time of year. She had placed aside her fair colors for shades of fate and strife. After all, the sun could not shine all of the time.

The swordsman rose and stepped close to her, causing her to flush in the warmth of his presence, much finer than fine yarn. "My captain released me from my vows to his daughter and bade me to go home until things settle. So I came here." He held out his hands. "If you'll have me."

Melisande placed her hands in his. "Well, the eaves could use some attention." She smiled.

She had not heard a mouse since humming to a kitchener stitch, of course. But as the swordsman took her into his arms, she remembered that pattern sense worked best through a gentle hand.

Curiosity

Curled up there on the threadbare rug a rusted, clockwork cat. Steel claws snagged within the cotton weave, purrs as scratchy echoes. Through cracked, grime-spat panes, curious flies, black wings dazzling in the broken sunlight descend upon the cat inching skittishly through its facial cogs seeking out the impossible odours of rancid flesh from within. Familiar feline contours, pyramidal ears, conal snout, and carbon fibre whiskers draw in the flies. Tick-sized brains deluded and lost to the delicious funk of rotted meat. Deep inside the funnels and flumes, of grills and copper coils, the flies search and slide on dusted, grease runs becoming trapped in the labyrinthine conduits of this once proud creation trapped within this peculiar clockwork flytrap. To a glutinous halt the flies slide against the fetid remains of the family of mice who once followed the hollow dream of a warm home. Outside, curious flies, black wings dazzling in the broken sunlight descend upon the cat inching skittishly through its facial cogs seeking out the impossible odours of rancid flesh from within.

— Neil Weston

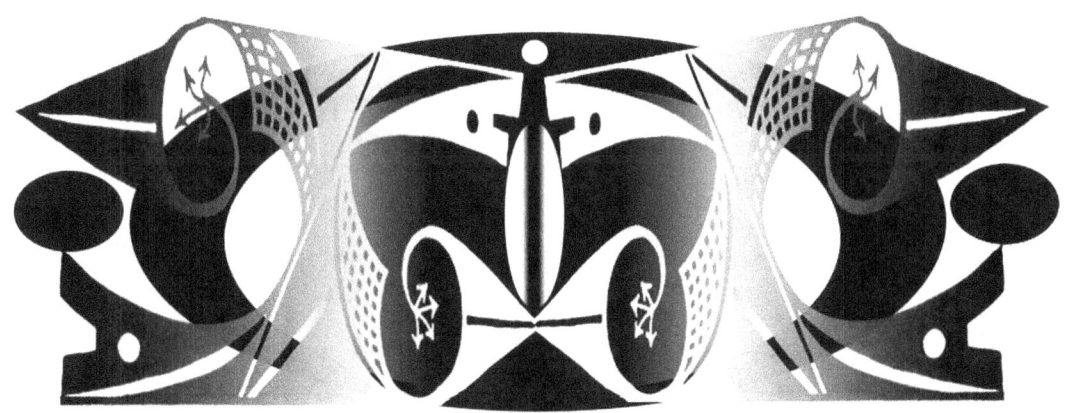

Big Monkey on Campus

Story by Patrick Thomas
Illustration by Paul Niemiec

It was clear to the Monkey King by his fourth week of college that not everyone shared his love of learning. It was especially apparent in classes simply from watching his fellow students sleep, text and most particularly the student who walked into class late, surrounded by a small army of zombie monkeys. And without offering an apology no less.

Sun WuKong sighed. They were just about to start talking about him before the disruption.

The professor, Ernest Bibble, was from the old school down to his tweed jacket with elbow patches, round spectacles, and tie with his university pin. Zombie monkeys or not, he was not one to suffer interruptions to his class lightly.

"Mr. Nurtle, you are late. Take your seat after leaving your pets outside," the gray-haired professor said in his crisp New England accent, the disdain he felt clear in every precisely enunciated syllable.

"They aren't pets. They're … service animals," Justin Nurtle replied, his disdain for the establishment, authority and everyone else who did not instantly bow down before his self-imagined greatness coming through just as clearly as his professor's. In fact, the opposing disdains seemed to be getting ready for a battle royal.

"I was unaware that you had a handicap requiring a service animal," Professor Bibble, his skepticism pushing aside his distain long enough for him to not outright call the student a liar.

"I'm training them for others," Nurtle said, expecting a teacher with three masters and a doctorate to ignore his common sense simply because Nurtle the great had told him otherwise.

"I will need to see Outré University approved permission. Do you have that paperwork, Mr. Nurtle?"

Nurtle made a show of touching all his pockets. "It must be in my other pants."

"Then I suggest you leave and make sure you are wearing the proper trousers when you return for my next class," Professor Bibble said.

"You're not letting me stay?" Nurtle said, his disbelief plainly apparent, although if asked, Nurtle would not be able to explain exactly a parent of what. He himself had been accused a time or two of being a parent in waiting by women he had had relations with. If asked, Nurtle would have advised disbelief to insist on proof via genetic testing before agreeing to any form of financial support.

"That is correct. Very astute. And to think some people think you only got into this university because your father is building the new biological research center building."

"You'll regret this old man," Nurtle promised.

"That is Professor Old Man to you. Now get out of my class before I am forced to call campus security."

Nurtle learned over and whispered to the zombie monkeys. Sun surmised correctly that this bunch had been raised in captivity. They appeared well fed, but had low muscle tone, even for zombies. All five were in the Rhesus family and each was less than two feet in height. And being dead, they didn't really have the few inhibitions normal monkeys did, so when Nurtle told them to grab the professors papers, glasses, car keys and such, the so-called zombie monkey army did not hesitate to wreck both havoc and the professor's lecture hall.

The notes for the class were thrown into the air and floated down like oddly shaped identical snowflakes. Eyeglasses were taken off Bibble's nose and the animated monkey corpse who stole the eyewear placed them on his own face, only to fall onto the floor. The coke bottle lens distorted the world too much for him to be able to judge distance correctly through undead eyes and brain. Another zombie simian began going through the professor's pockets, removing gum, a handkerchief and some condoms—which made the professor's normal pale complexion become rosy—before finally locating the keys and running toward the parking lot by way of an open window.

The last zombie monkey climbed up the professor's back like the older man was a tree with rotten bananas waiting at the top. The dead primate stood on Bibble's shoulders and pulled the hair on top of the man's head. Nurtle had assumed it was a toupee when in reality the teacher just had a horribly bad haircut, which explained why it was not coming off. Instead of a hairpiece, the furry little zombie was yanking hair and scalp off the old man's head.

In his very long life, the Monkey King had done much—fought monsters, destroyed a pantheon of gods, and even saved the world on occasion, but he had never been to college. So far it had proved to be an enlightening experience and from the looks of things was about to get far more interesting. Among the human people of China, wishing that someone live in interesting times was considered a curse. Sun WuKong never understood the negative connotations. Then again, he was the one usually making things interesting.

The disrupted class was better than the rest

of his courses—more so than the Joy of Garbage or Quantum Physics. Sun was quite disappointed when he found out Taking Marx Seriously wasn't about Groucho, Harpo and Chico and that he did not have to be submerged for Underwater Basket Weaving, only the straw did.

Tricksters in Myth, Literature, and Modern Society—this class—was by far his favorite, especially today. Professor Bibble was starting his second day of lectures on *Journey to the West*. As Sun was the undisputed star of said book, the Monkey King was paying rapt attention. The teacher didn't even mind him interrupting the previous class with insights, especially since Sun was able to quote different versions and translations as well as the oral tradition and do it in multiple languages.

Not only had Nurtle interrupted this very special class, but he was stopping the rest of the students from learning more about the Monkey King's exploits. Worse, he was taking advantage of dead monkeys to do it. It simply could not be tolerated. Sun stood, a hooded sweatshirt covering his head, and went to the professor's aide in an attempt to stop the zombie monkey who was endeavoring to make the old man bald and bloody.

"Stop this now," commanded the Monkey King. The zombie monkey ignored him, instead yanking another handful of gray hair. This was unusual as most living monkeys had an inborn ability to recognize and obey their king.

Sun reached out and caught each of the zombie monkey's hands. Humans might say paws, but there were opposable thumbs which is what made a hand as far as Sun was concerned.

"Let me help you get that monkey off your back, Professor," Sun said as he gently lifted the zombie simian off his teacher, making sure he held it close so it couldn't get away.

"Thank you, Mr. Simia," Bibble said, straightening his tweed jacket in an attempt to recover his lost dignity. He checked his pockets, but his dignity wasn't there. Next he touched the top of his head and winced. No dignity there either. Plenty of blood and missing hair though.

"Please, call me Rex," the Monkey King in human disguise said.

None of this set well with Nurtle. "Who do you think you are to touch my monkey?"

"I think the better question is who do you think you are for doing this to innocent monkeys?" Sun said.

"I'm the zombie monkey king," said Nurtle.

"And they are my army."

Now much time had passed for Sun WuKong since the events chronicled in *Journey to the West*. He liked to think that in the ensuing centuries he had grown and was not as prone to fits of anger over small insults. And the truth was, he had and was not. In his younger days, this self-proclaimed zombie monkey king would not be standing. But Sun was a better monkey now. That didn't mean the insult would go unanswered.

"You claim to be on par with the great Sun WuKong?"

"Who?" Nurtle asked.

"Excuse me?" Sun said. "You don't know who the Monkey King is? Didn't you play attention in the last class or even read ahead in your syllabus?"

"Duh. Who would do that?" Nurtle said. "Some geek maybe."

"Then why would you declare yourself a king of monkeys?" Sun said.

"Why? Look at me—I have raised these monkeys from the dead and made them my slaves."

"Slavery is bad. Especially for monkeys," said Sun.

"Who cares about a bunch of dead monkeys?" Nurtle said.

"I do," Sun replied.

"Then you're an idiot," Nurtle said.

Sun smiled. "We shall see who the idiot is. But I am fair. Issue a simple apology and lay these monkeys back down to rest and I am willing to forget the whole matter. And Professor Bibble can get back to teaching about the true Monkey King."

"Like anyone cares about that," Nurtle said. "Zombie monkeys are stronger than people. Now let go of my monkey or I'll have him hurt you."

"You are not getting your slave back. Even a dead monkey deserves better than that," Sun said.

"Your funeral. Get him!"

The zombie monkey went wild, clawing and biting at Sun, but the Monkey King's skin, even transformed as he was into a human, was so hard it broke the poor creatures' nails and teeth. But it gave the Monkey King an idea. Most people thought a bite from a zombie made more zombies. That was not the case, but that ignorance was something Sun could use to his advantage.

Sun dropped the zombie monkey and grabbed his own arm, screaming in pain. "It bit me! It bit me!"

"I told you not to mess with me, Rex," Nurtle said, a smug look settled so firmly across his face that it would take a crowbar to pry it off. That or perhaps a few smacks from said crowbar.

"What's happening to me?" Sun fell to the floor convulsing and twitching, guilty of the sin of overacting. Nurtle didn't seem to notice. "Somebody help me!" Sun continued to move like he was having a seizure, rolling back and forth across the floor so he ended up by Nurtle's feet. Grabbing hold of the self-proclaimed zombie monkey king's pant leg, Sun looked up and let his true form shine through. Nurtle ended up staring into the face of a man-size monkey. Nurtle's pupils grew to the point where they seemed to swallow his irises whole. Then Sun further transformed, making his flesh look rotten and rancid.

It was Nurtle's turn to scream as he kicked frantically, trying to get free of the Monkey King's grasp. Sun held on long enough to induce panic. When Nurtle started weeping like a baby, Sun let go of his leg, but held onto his shoe. The loss of footwear was acceptable to the college student as he ran toward the door of the lecture hall. Nurtle did pause once to look back. Sun was on his feet, arms outstretched and lurching like a movie zombie.

"Brains," Sun moaned, lumbering toward Nurtle.

"Stop him, my monkeys! Stop him now!" he screamed and ran out of the lecture hall.

The four remaining zombie monkeys did as they were told which made Sun very sad. His monkey kingdom was long gone, but he still felt a kinship to modern day simians. Being a minion was no way to spend a life, even an undead one. Sun could see into the infrared, ultraviolet and magic spectrums. These monkeys had been dead long before they were raised. Their souls had departed, which was a blessing. A soul trapped in its own corpse is rarely a pleasant thing.

Although it made him quite unhappy, Sun knew he had to stop his little undead brothers. The zombie monkeys were several times stronger than a human and could break bones or kill someone, even if the worst their bites would really do is cause an infection or rend flesh.

Depending on the type of magic that animated the furry corpses, crushing the cerebellum should at least make it difficult for them to move. Sun was likely the greatest martial artist on the planet—he acknowledged the possibility, however slight, of there being someone more skilled than he was. It was a simple matter for Sun to ram his index finger through the back of four tiny skulls and wiggle it around to destroy their motor centers.

This didn't stop them from moving, although they were unable to stand upright or walk in a straight line. It was enough to make sure they couldn't hurt any of his fellow students or Professor Bibble.

"Rex, are you all right?" Bibble asked, genuine concern overriding his typical manner of formal address.

Sun's hoodie still covered his face, so no one but Nurtle had seen him transform. Sun slid back into his human Rex Simia guise before facing his teacher.

"I'm fine, Professor Bibble. Just giving Nurtle a taste of his own medicine," Sun said, picking up the eyeglasses from the face of the fallen zombie monkey who had taken them and handing them back to their rightful owner.

The professor put the spectacles back on his nose and moved closer to get a better look. "Those really are zombie monkeys, aren't they?"

Sun nodded, surprised at how readily Bibble accepted the truth. Most humans seemed to have an innate ability to ignore or explain away the mystical. It raised the man up a notch in Sun's opinion and he had been fairly high to begin with due to three brilliant papers he had published on *Journey to the West*.

"Five isn't much of an army, is it?" Bibble said.

"No, it isn't," Sun agreed.

"How did you frighten him off? And how did you stop his so-called army?"

"It's something I'd rather not discuss right now," Sun said. He had enjoyed his anonymity and having people treat him as if he was just a regular college student. It was a nice change and the Monkey King had hoped to at least finish out the semester, especially since he wouldn't get his dorm room or tuition money back. Not that it was his money—he was at Outré on several scholarships which actually paid out more than all his expenses, but it was the principle of the thing. "I'll take care of the monkeys, but I have one request."

"What is it, Mr. Simia?"

"Would you please hold off on your Monkey King lecture until the next class?"

Bibble smiled. "I think I can do that. What about Mr. Nurtle?"

"Oh, I'll be taking care of him too," Sun said.

"Be careful. His father has connections," Bibble said. "Dangerous ones."

"I'll keep that in mind," the Monkey King said, when in truth the warning didn't even make it in one ear in order to go out the other. Instead, Sun blocked it before it could even enter his mind and knocked it to the ground to be trampled beneath his hairy feet and toes.

Sun took a black trash bag from a garbage can and tenderly loaded the four monkeys inside of it. The bag of dead monkeys writhed clumsily as he threw it over his shoulder and walked out onto the campus.

When choosing his body shape and size for his Rex Simia persona, Sun made himself about average height with an athletic build. He made his features a mix, so depending on the angle he could appear to be of Asian or European descent. Human descent that is. Europe had no native monkeys to speak of. Their loss. But no matter his shape, the Monkey King had trouble hiding his smile and his sense of humor. It had made him very popular on campus.

Even as he carried the black bag of zombie simians, people called out his name and he returned their greetings. Only a month into the semester and he was a big man on campus. He'd rather have been the big monkey on campus, but that would have made his student career far more complicated than Sun wanted.

A couple of giggling girls saw what he was carrying and walked alongside him.

"Hey Rex, what's in the bag?" the blonde, whose name was Trish, asked.

"Zombie monkeys," he replied, which caused much giggling to ensue.

"Are you going to the Digamma Psi kegger?"

"Wouldn't miss it," Sun said.

"Is it true they want you to pledge?' Trish asked.

Sun shrugged. "They asked."

"You gonna?" she said.

"Haven't decided."

As they neared the parking lot, an alarm was going off. It was something that was typically ignored and might have been overlooked this time too if not for the deceased primate piloting the vehicle at breathtaking speeds.

"Was a monkey driving that car?" Trish asked.

"I guess anyone can get a driver's license these days. See you at the party," Sun said, racing after the sedan.

For a zombie monkey, the little fellow was driving amazingly well. Sure, he rode over a lawn and went the wrong way down a one-way street, but so far hadn't hit anything except the horn. Repeatedly. He must have liked the noise, but the sound combined with the blaring alarm encouraged people to get out of his way.

Sun ran alongside the car, reached in the driver's window and turned the car engine off, which

might have stopped the car if it hadn't just crested the top of a very steep hill. It was also a standard, making the dead primate's accomplishment in getting it moving that much more impressive.

The car picked up speed with Sun's arm still inside. If nobody was watching, he could have easily stopped the car. However, plenty of people were looking on in interest, many of whom might wonder why Rex Simia had the muscle power to stop a speeding sedan. To further complicate matters, it was a beautiful sunny day and the hill was near a lawn where students liked to lay out, play hackie sack, toss a Frisbee and text, so Sun had an audience of over a hundred. The stickiest wicket was the delivery truck coming up the other side of the hill, going in the correct direction on the one-way street.

Sun used his arm to steer the car off to his right in hopes the truck driver would do the same in the opposite direction. The driver did, but the road was narrow. There wasn't going to be enough room for him to pass untouched between the vehicles and people would definitely start talking if Rex was unhurt, but the side of the truck was smashed in.

Sun waited until the last minute, then flipped himself up into a hand stand position on the car door. The truck passed with only a blowing of its horn. The zombie monkey blew his horn in reply as if it were a moose answering a mating call. The car finally rolled to a stop and Sun eased it into an open parking spot.

People were pointing many things at him—fingers, hands and of course, cell phones. The stunt would likely be posted on YouTube within the hour.

With the car stopped, the last zombie monkey ran out the open window, across the street and into the crowd.

"Come back here," Sun ordered, but the dead monkey ignored him and instead began throwing books, purses and a small dog into the air.

Sun managed to catch the dog and safely return him to the ground, which gave the zombie monkey the chance to run up the side of a building.

The Monkey King could have leapt to the roof in a single bound to cut him off, but again it would have ended Rex's college career.

Instead, Sun picked up a rock and flicked it with his wrist. The stone traveled with such velocity that when it struck the climber, it knocked the furry zombie off the building. Sun was already running and was right underneath it with the black garbage bag open. Zombie monkey number five fell right in and joined zombie monkeys one through four. Sun closed the bag and took off across campus.

Many people looked on with confused interest, but nobody followed. Sun headed to the construction site of the new biology building. The area was sectioned off from the campus by a wooden fence, which Sun scaled with ease using only his feet. The foundation for the basement was already poured and there was one section marked off for the septic system that seemed sturdy enough, so Sun dumped zombie monkeys one through four in, stopping to lobotomize number five before dropping him too in the cement hole. Sun then dragged a slab of concrete that weighed tons and put it over the top so the zombie monkeys couldn't get out. They were strong, but not strong enough to move something that heavy.

It was time to deal with Nurtle. The Monkey King was stronger and could simply pound the living daylights out of his fellow student, but where was the fun in that? Sun may have grown since the events in *Journey to the West*, but he was still all about the fun.

Sun carefully plucked five hairs from his arm and put them into his mouth, chewing carefully. Moments later he spat the hairs out, but they never hit the ground. Instead each transformed into replicas of the quintet of the so-called zombie monkey army.

Sun was able to turn each of his hairs into a duplicate of himself, but the more bodies he made, the more difficult they were to control. Splitting his focus and concentration six ways was a challenge, but not quite as difficult as understanding the logic that Nurtle used to start his so-called army.

The five selves went off to Nurtle's dorm room, where they found him curled up in a closet.

They opened the door and Nurtle screamed. When nothing happened, he opened up his eyes long enough to see it was only his zombies come home. Slowly, he stood up and searched the room. They were alone. Nurtle crept up to the dorm room door and peaked outside, looking left and right. Nobody was there.

Nurtle sighed, wiped his brow and went back into his room, only to turn and see the zombie monkey version of Rex Simia standing there.

"Brains," he whispered.

Nurtle spun and ran, smashing his face into the half closed door. His fear took control, forcing him to try to see through the stars that were floating in front of his eyes and escape from the dorm room. Nurtle fled, his imitation zombie monkey army following close behind as he left the dorm and sprinted across the quad to the dining hall. Only then did he look behind him, wheezing from the exertion. Rex was nowhere to be found.

Nurtle realized people were staring, so he stood up in an attempt to regain his composure. Composure proved to be elusive as he was still missing his one shoe. If anyone asked, he'd say he was starting a new style. Then he'd figure out a way to lose Rex Simia. He could always call his father, but that would be a last resort. Carl Nurtle had no respect for his offspring, barely tolerating his own flesh and blood. Plus, he might be upset if he found out his son had taken the obsidian dagger from his office to raise dead monkeys from the anatomy lab.

The zombie monkey army seemed like such a good idea three days ago. It got him into the hottest club in town. When the bouncers tried to stop him, he just had his monkeys push them aside. Turns out drunk women, or at least one particular lady of the Goth variety, loved zombie monkeys and he had gotten more action in the last seventy-two hours than he had in six months. Sober women without multiple body piercings were apparently less enamored and more terrified, but that was all right because they were giving Nurtle respect. As were the guys. Before the zombie monkey army came into his life, he didn't have many close friends. He blamed everyone else for that. The reasons he ascribed varied between people being unable to see his true greatness or being so jealous of said greatness that they couldn't stand to be around him. Sure people hung out with him because of who his father was, but that never seemed to last. On the plus side, bullies steered clear of him, afraid of retribution by his father's men.

Now things were different. People were more afraid of him than they were of his father and it was great. It would have stayed that way too if the stupid monkey hadn't gone and bitten Simia.

Nurtle decided he was more hungry than scared, so he got in line, ordering his zombie monkeys to get his tray and glass for him. He enjoyed the apprehension in the faces of the food service workers. It was almost enough to forget about Simia. Nurtle made his way through the line, grabbing some French fries and an apple. When Nurtle got to the hot food section, the serving lady had her head down so all he could see was her hair net. Nurtle figured she was probably too afraid to meet his eyes and felt empowered.

"You make sure I get double normal portions, you hear? What's the special today?"

"Meatloaf." The server looked up and she wasn't a lady or human. The now familiar face that greeted him was furry and had pieces of raw flesh hanging off which made the smile in the center of it all that much more disturbing. "Made of brains."

Nurtle left so fast he didn't notice one of his imitation zombie monkeys had untied his good shoe and removed it as he fled the cafeteria.

Nurtle made his way back to his room to again huddle in his closet, his zombie monkeys surrounding him like statues, doing nothing but stare at him. Then one covered his mouth with his hands. Another, his ears. The next, his eyes. The fourth his butt and the last stuck a finger up his right nostril. Nurtle nervously closed the closet door so he didn't have to look at them. Hours passed until the sun had set. Then there was a knock at his door.

"Who is it?" No answer. "I said who is it?" Still no answer, only a scratching on the wood.

Nurtle exited the closet and started tying his sheets together, fastened them to his bed, then shimmied down from his second story window. While not deserted, there weren't many people out on campus, so he ran in his stocking feet toward the student union in hopes that there might be safety in a crowd. Taking a shortcut between two buildings turned out to be a bad idea because Rex Simia was standing there waiting for him. Nurtle turned around to head back the way he came, but Rex moved fast enough to somehow get in front of him.

"Leave me alone!"

"I can't. You did this to me, made me into this creature. Tell me, how did you do it?" Sun asked in a deep, moaning voice.

"I'm not going to tell you anything. I'll send my zombie monkeys against you again if you don't back off."

"It is too late for that. You have tampered with forbidden magic and now must pay the price. The monkeys and I are now bound together. If fact, we are becoming one," Sun said, his mouth opening far too wide, for more than a human or monkey jaw ought to be able to manage. One of the imitation dead simians leapt up into the air and landed in the mouth of what Nurtle thought was a zombie were-monkey.

Rex Simia grew as tall as a professional basketball player. He got bigger still when zombie monkeys two, three, and four did the same. Rex was now taller than the nearby lamppost.

The last of the monkeys climbed up the lamppost and swung over into the giant zombie monkey's open mouth. Rex Simia roared and grew even larger, his clothes tearing.

The giant looked down at Nurtle. "You know what I want?"

"Brains?" Nurtle whispered.

"Yeah, but with you it that'd only be an appetizer, so I may have to devour the rest of you too. Tell me how you raised those monkeys from the dead and maybe I'll leave your brain in your head," Sun said.

"No, I won't let you eat me," Nurtle said, running yet again, this time to what would soon be the old biology building. Taking steps three at a time, he ended up on the fifth floor in the lab that had been the original resting place of the monkeys.

Nurtle's chest heaved as he ducked behind a wooden lab table. "I'm safe in here. He's too big to get in." Then Nurtle felt a breeze. It was warm and it seemed to be going in and out of the window, almost in rhythm with his own breathing. Slowly he turned his head, only to see a single giant monkey eye and a nostril outside the open floor to ceiling window.

"Want to bet?" was the giant zombie monkey's reply as two humungous fingers reached in and pulled Nurtle out. The student looked down at the pavement fifty feet below and thought the drop was the most terrifying thing he had ever seen. Then he looked up at the face of the true monkey king and soiled himself.

"Tell me how you did it," Sun demanded. Without that knowledge, he'd never be able to lay the real monkeys back down to rest.

"No," Nurtle screamed in defiance. "I won't."

"Okeydokey," Sun said, lifting the young man up so he dangled over his huge mouth and gullet. "Snack time."

Sun pretended to drop him, but it was the giant tongue licking humongous monkey lips and teeth that finally broke Nurtle. "I'll tell you. I used a special blade. You stick it in something dead and it comes back as a zombie that has to listen to you as long as the knife's touching your skin."

"Where is this knife?" Sun's voice boomed.

Nurtle brought his ankle up to his hands and pulled out a blade from a sheath under his pant leg. "Here. Take it. Just don't eat me. Please."

Sun took the tiny blade between the giant index finger and thumb of his free hand.

"Hmm, I seem to recall you saying something about Sun WuKong the Monkey King being stupid and nobody caring about his stories. I didn't like that one bit. In fact, it upset me greatly."

"The Monkey King is the greatest and his book is the best one ever," Nurtle said without stammering despite the trembling that was shaking the rest of his body.

"Now was that so hard?"

Nurtle ignored the question to ask one of his own. "Are you going to eat me?"

"Probably, but since you were so cooperative, I'll give you a head start," Sun said, setting the young man on the ground.

"How much of a head start?" Nurtle asked.

"Not enough for you to waste some of it by standing there and asking stupid questions."

For someone who had never even thought about joining a track team, Nurtle was getting a lot of running time in. His sock-clad feet took him toward the student union. He dared one glance over his shoulder to see the giant zombie monkey running after him.

Nurtle didn't need to look again, because he could feel the ground shake from each step of the humongous creature chasing him.

Nurtle burst into the student union, noticed a crowd in the main ballroom and ran inside.

"You have to help me! I'm being chased by Rex Simia. He's a giant zombie monkey, bigger than King Kong," Nurtle said. A large man put a beefy hand on his shoulder and spun him around. "Dad?"

"Justin, what are you babbling about? And why are you late for the dinner to celebrate the new building? Where is your tux? And your shoes?"

Nurtle had totally forgotten about the banquet, but not about what was chasing him.

"Dad, you have to help me."

"Against the giant monkey?" Carl Nurtle replied, his tone dark and dry.

A man in a tuxedo joined them. "What is your son going on about?"

"Justin, you remember James Nixon, president of Outré University."

"Dad, you have to help me. Do something. Shoot him."

"Young man, we have a strict no weapons policy at this university. Who did you say is chasing you?"

"Rex Simia."

"Rex is one of our most promising freshmen," Nixon said. "He has earned a record number of scholarships."

"No, he's a giant zombie monkey and he wants to eat my brain," Nurtle said.

"Actually, I'm pretty sure I'd still be hungry after a meal that small," Sun said, back in his human Rex Simia form. His latest shape shift had traded up from his hoodie to a black tuxedo with matching bow tie.

"Unfortunately, I'm inclined to agree with you," Carl Nurtle said, glaring daggers at his son.

"Rex, do you know what Justin Nurtle is talking about?" Nixon asked.

"Sounds like a pretty wild story to me, sir," Sun said. "But no hard feelings."

Sun extended his hand.

Justin Nurtle took it warily. Sun leaned to playfully slap his shoulder and said in a whisper just loud enough for the younger Nurtle to hear, "Brains."

Justin Nurtle pulled his hand away and slugged Rex on the chin. It wasn't much of a punch, but the Monkey King made like it was and took a dive.

Sun started to his feet, maneuvering to his right where no one could see his face but the younger Nurtle and he mouthed the word "sucker." Then he stuck his tongue out. Nurtle's anger overcame his fear and common sense and led a rush forward in an attempt at a tackle as Rex was standing back up. Unfortunately for him, Sun stepped aside and spun at the last instant so Nurtle instead ended up knocking the university president to the ground.

"Justin, we do not tolerate this behavior at Outré University. You have just attacked another student and a faculty member. The bylaws of the university are clear," President Nixon said, as Sun helped him to his feet. "I'm sorry Carl, but your son is suspended until there can be a hearing for his expulsion."

"What?" Nurtle the younger shouted. "Do you have any idea who you're talking to? You are going to be sorry…"

"Justin, shut up," his father said softly, his whisper carrying more authority than most men's shouts.

"But Dad…"

"Not another word. Go home. Now," Carl Nurtle said.

The younger Nurtle fumed, but didn't dare argue with his father. Men who did that disappeared. With a single glare at Rex Simia, he left.

"Rex, are you okay?" Nixon asked.

Sun rubbed his jaw. "I'm fine, sir."

"If you want to press charges…"

"I don't think that will be necessary," Sun said with a grin.

"Jim, is there anything that can be done?" Carl Nurtle asked.

James Nixon sighed. "Carl, you've been a great friend to both me and this university, but your son is a loose cannon. I was going to speak to you tonight because I had a complaint about your son using trained monkeys to attack one of his teachers."

"Justin isn't bright enough to train a goldfish, let alone something with legs," Carl Nurtle said.

"Be that as it may, your son attacked Rex and me in front of witnesses." President Nixon pointed to a group with video cameras and cell phones pointed their way. "And the student television station is doing a live webcast. If I don't go by the book, the whole thing will go viral and they'll have my job. I'm truly sorry."

"I understand," Carl Nurtle said in a tone that indicated that he didn't. "I think I'll be leaving. Pity I have the last check for the building in my pocket. I guess we'll just have to cancel the ceremony during dessert where I was to present it to you." President Nixon opened his mouth to protest, but was cut off. "Goodnight Jim, Mr. Simia."

Carl Nurtle turned and walked away. Two large men fell in behind him, either of which at first glance could have been mistaken for an ape in a suit. The university president gritted his teeth, but turned to visit with other banquet guests.

Sun circled the room, then moved toward the buffet table. Professor Bibble strolled over to join him.

"So you got everything sorted out then?" Bibble asked.

"Pretty much. I still have to lay the monkeys back to rest," Sun said.

"Translation, make them all the way dead," Bibble said.

"Yes."

Bibble nodded sagely and took a bite of brie. "You know your name is very interesting."

"Is it?" Sun said, raising an eyebrow.

"Yes. Loosely translated from bad Latin, do you know it means King Monkey?" Bibble said. "Or Monkey King."

"Interesting," Sun said.

"And apparently there have been some very interesting stories going around campus. For one thing, my car was apparently stolen by one of the zombie monkeys, but a very interesting video on YouTube showed me just where to find it. And several people at the party are actually backing up Mr. Nurtle the younger's wild tale, saying that they too saw a giant zombie monkey on campus, lurking outside the old biology building."

"But no video," Sun said with a smile.

"Apparently too dark. Whatever it was, it either avoided bright areas or somehow turned off lights."

"A pity," Sun said.

"Anything else you would like to add?" the professor asked.

"Nope, I'm good," Sun said, still unable to hide his infectious smile.

Bibble and the disguised Sun WuKong shared a look. The professor took a banana off the table and handed it to his student.

"I think I will find the rest of your insights on *The Journey to the West* more enlightening than even I expected," Bibble said.

Sun pealed the banana and took a bite. "You might at that."

calling all creators

is this the common run of days
a figment of the brain

as the parade of perpetrators
stumble in the rain

what if imagination
is all that keeps us sane

— Anna Sykora

This autumn, explore of the worlds of mad science with *Tales of the Talisman!*

The Large Hadron Collider provides scientists an opportunity to test predictions made by particle and high-energy physics. Lee Clark Zumpe shows us what could happen if an elder god chose to use it as a gateway.

Charles Chapman and David Van Houten imagine scientists building an artificial heart in the nineteenth century to pulse-pounding and maddening effect.

In the future, the wealthy might have the ability to reinact the space flights of the 60s. Mike Wilson shows us that such games are not without peril.

Erin K. Wagner asks what would have happened if Thomas Edison had used his inventions to summon the dead.

Indulge your weird scientific curiosity with these and other stories this autumn in *Tales of the Talisman!*

Don't miss a single issue, subscribe to *Tales of the Talisman* at www.talesofthetalisman.com today!

One year $24.00 (That's 25% off the cover price)
Back issues available for $8.00 apiece

Visit hadrosaur.com for more great books and audio available from Hadrosaur Productions

Subscriptions also available by mail at:

Hadrosaur Productions, P.O. Box 2194, Mesilla Park, NM 88047-2194

Moonglow
A Starwisp Cycle Story

Story by Edward J. McFadden III
Illustration by Erika McGinnis

1

The balloons floated listlessly in the fog. They had lost their baskets, and all of them had been torn, and were almost deflated, the breeze spinning and lifting them like deformed marionettes. The leather basket tethers trailed behind the forlorn balloons, hanging through the fog-like tentacles dangling from enormous dead octopuses.

Sayzar lay on the hardpan, watching his money sail away on the breeze. Moonglow started in six cycles, and now they had to walk to Bonetown, which was thirty leagues east. Sayzar got up, brushed himself off with his hat, and placed the large purple fedora back atop his head. A white feather stuck in the hat's lapel, along with a thin copper tube that ran to the edge of the hat's brim, and hooked over the edge. During a rain, the tube provided drinking water.

Sayzar's leg hurt, but nothing was broken. He looked around, took out his spyglass, and surveyed the area. He saw Pam and Krispin walking toward him away from their destroyed basket, and as he arced the spyglass across the horizon, he saw Damroth and Taeda sitting up and rubbing dust from their eyes. A balloon basket lay in front of them and was still smoldering.

He turned 360 degrees and didn't see Pathina. It was bad enough that they had crashed their balloons, but if they lost her that would just top things off. Desolate hardpan stretched in every direction, broken occasionally by a tuft of scrub pine, a giant rock, or a mesa. They had come east with the wind, cutting across the Chasm of Time, and floating northeast over the edge of Tanglewood Forest. That left them in the Wasted Lands, Sayzar was sure of it.

The fog had been so thick they had flown into a huge mesa like the ones in Hollowhaven Valley to the north. When they hit the mesa, fuel from the fires they used to inflate their great balloons had spilled, and the baskets, leather harnesses, supplies, and huge wind rudders caught fire. The party had barely escaped death by releasing their balloons as they neared the hardpan, crashing to ground in their baskets like balls of flame.

Wind swept across the barren plane, and when Pam and Krispin arrived, Sayzar saw that Pathina was with them, and had somehow avoided his spyglass. "Oy," said Krispin. "What the hell was that?"

"I didn't know there were mesas out here," said Sayzar. "There's nothing on my map."

Damroth arrived with Taeda, and he dropped his pack, and collapsed to the ground exhausted. Thankfully, no one had been hurt. "Don't get too comfortable. Without the balloons we have to hoof it the rest of the way. Bonetown is an easy thirty leagues still."

Pathina said, "Are you sure we didn't change direction somehow when we crossed the Chasm of Time?"

Sayzar looked at the ratty old women, but checked his anger. If he was to have the flute, he needed her. "These are the Wasted Lands, no?"

Pathina drew out a brass device and flipped open the lid, tossing aside her long gray-black hair as she did so. An X marked with an S, N, E, and W, floated in thick green liquid, and Pathina placed the device in the palm of her aged hand, holding it steady. She twisted a knob that turned a series of cogs that caused the X to spin, and her emerald eyes danced as she watched it. When finally it stopped, Pathina said, "That way is east. Bonetown," she said, pointing over Sayzar's shoulder.

Damroth looked at Pam and Krispin. The three of them were really only hired help on this trip, and Sayzar surmised that they were considering taking their leave of the party. They had no starwisp magic, and no way of knowing whether the moonglow would give them a skill, and if it did, what that skill would be. They were thinking the walk to Dusktown was much shorter.

The starwisps came for one night every thirty-three cycles, and upon their arrival, those lucky enough to have been touched got their magic back for nineteen hours, or one single cycle. Every time the starwisps came, a new group of people would be chosen and rewarded with magic to replace those who had died, or simply lost their gift. The magic manifested itself as a unique skill, some of which were one of a kind, and some of which duplicated, like the ability to heal.

Taeda was the only member of their group to have traditional starwisp magic, but Sayzar had sworn her to secrecy about what her skill was. Sayzar had told everyone in the party different stories, and the only one who knew the entire plan was Pathina, who was part magician, part seer, and part earth mother, and she was to be their guide when they got to Bonetown. She also said she'd be able to do something pretty miraculous during moonglow, if her family history could be trusted.

Moonglow only came once every 7,019 cycles,

when three large moons filled the sky and the sun's rays reflected off the spheres creating three cycles of no full darkness. At night, during moonglow, a gray haze pervaded the land, but it never got dark. During the haze, many people who didn't have starwisp magic got a special skill just for moonglow, sort of a special treat for those who had been passed over by the starwisps.

The starwisps hadn't come during a moonglow in more than an epoch.

Sayzar believed that this rare event would strengthen, and expand a person's starwisp magic, and that when the starwisps came they would have an even greater, more unique power, and that's what his plan was based on. He looked at Damroth, Pam, and Krispin, and said, "Look, I know things haven't worked out so far, but stay with me. There is a pot of gold at the end of the tunnel."

"Perhaps if you told us what we were searching for?" said Damroth. The big man was pure muscle, nothing else. He had lost half his face in a knife fight, and that section of his head was covered with a brass plate molded to his skull, covering one eye socket.

"In due time," he said, and before long they were done scavenging what gear they could, and were traipsing along the hardpan in an even line to hide their number. He would tell them about the flute, but he wouldn't do that until they were all under its spell.

2

They made camp the third night two leagues from Bonetown's entrance, because Bonetown was the kind of place you didn't want to enter at night. They started no fire, but huddled behind a tall rock out of the wind, a brass heatstone on the ground between them. The breeze carried the faint scent of pine, and off to the south they saw the edge of Tanglewood Forest, a thin line of green cutting through the bleakness of the Wasted Lands.

Sayzar wanted to tell the group about his plan, but once he did they won't need him anymore. A Crankit howled in the distance, and Sayzar was reminded of the time he had been attacked by the large, humanoid-like creatures covered in black fur. They hid in the hardpan underground, and attacked unsuspecting victims as they approached.

Sayzar lit a smoke, and walked away from the camp, signaling Taeda to follow him. Taeda could read and understand any language when her starwisp magic came, and that was the key to his entire plan, but he didn't want the group to know that just yet.

Sayzar considered what he should tell Taeda. In Bonetown there was a paragraph of verse carved into a great slab of bone that was said to reveal the location of Izril's flute, an instrument allegedly made of bone, and that when played within earshot of someone who got magic when the starwisps came, got their magic back for as long as they heard the flute's music. The flute would make him rich beyond anything he could have possibility dreamed. When the starwisps left, the magic left the land for thirty-three cycles, but with the flute, he could help people do magic every cycle.

"Yeah," said Taeda, and another Crankit howl pierced the night. Taeda looked over her shoulder, and said, "They're getting closer, Sayzar."

"Not to worry. Listen, I just wanted to talk to you alone for a bit." Taeda nodded in the darkness, her outline clear against the bright moonlight. With moonglow only three cycles away, the night sky was already starting to lighten. "I need you to understand why I'm keeping my plan secret."

Taeda nodded, and said, "I know you don't trust us, boss."

"Not true," said Sayzar. "I trust you, and Patina, but we need the others for a bit longer, until we're done in Bonetown."

"You afraid Damroft, Pam and Krispin will strike off on their own once they know where the flute is, and beat you to it?"

"Or that they'll sell the information. We only have three cycles until Moonglow, and once that starts, things in Bonetown could get a bit hairy," said Sayzar.

There was screaming coming from the camp, and Taeda and Sayzar heard growling, and the panicked cries of Pat. Sayzar pulled his pistola, a cylindrical brass device that discharged rocks and metal shot via a series of springs and cogs that spit the projectile from the tube. The weapon only had a range of fifteen feet or so, but could put down a large animal from that distance.

Taeda drew her knife, as Sayzar opened a bag that dangled from his waist containing round metal shot and rocks. When they arrived back at camp Pam and Krispin were surrounded by eight Crankits, creatures that some said had been created by the mixed breading of people and the wolfins that lived in the Racket Mountains by the South Falls.

Sayzar shot one of the beasts and it cried out, turning its large snoot and glaring eyes on him. He reloaded and was firing again in seconds, and the distraction allowed Damroth to move in with his large broadsword, and he hacked and cleaved his way toward Pam and Krispin until only half of the beasts were left standing.

Pathina had her back to the large rock, her knife held before her as she watched the scene in panic. Her cloak let her blend into the night, and though the animals smelled her, they could barely see her. Several minutes passed as Damroth and Sayzar cleared out the creatures, and when there was only one left, it bolted into the darkness, looking back several times as if to say "I'll be back with friends."

"Everyone OK," asked Sayzar. Krispin had a small cut on his right arm, but other than that, no one had been hurt. "Consider yourself lucky that it wasn't a bigger pack. Sometimes they attack in groups of fifty or more."

"You think he's going to get his friends?" asked Pathina.

"I do," said Sayzar. "Pack your stuff. We're heading out." The thought of walking across the Wasted Lands at night brought a series of terrible images to Sayzar's mind, but what choice did they have? They couldn't risk another attack, and they still had a ways to go before they got to Bonetown.

The sun was coming up when they saw the tall sand dunes that surrounded the spiral entrance to Bonetown. "We'll break here until full light and eat," said Sayzar, a smile creeping across his face.

3

The entrance to Bonetown was a long spiral road that led down into a deep sand crater. Two tall statues depicting the huge beasts that had once come to die there flanked both sides of a wooden gate that stood open. The road ran around the edges of the hole, and at its bottom, people of various races and professions lived in the skeletons of long extinct animals.

The giant skeletons were larger than mesas, some stretching as long as 500 feet and as tall as fifty. Clear tissue that had hardened to bone covered huge rib cages, and within these large covered spaces there were communities that made their homes in the carved out appendages and skulls. Nineteen skeletons made up the bulk of Bonetown, and almost everything other than the sand of the Wasted Lands was in one way or another made of bone.

No one knew how long ago the giant beasts had lived, but the graveyard had served the destitute and desperate for so long that a thriving civilization called the place home, importing most of their food and supplies using credits raised by their bone sculptures and other bone products, like sword hilts, jewelry, tools, and a myriad of other things that couldn't be found anywhere else in the world.

Sayzar paused briefly at the gate, studying the statues, and eyeing the road. "Things can get crazy from here. There is no ruler of Bonetown, and thus no rule of law. We are on our own. Keep your eyes peeled and your weapons at the ready." Sayzar pulled free his propulsion gun, and held it by his side.

They saw other people as soon as they started down the road. Vendors selling various wares dotted the side of the path, and the party stopped occasionally, being friendly, but didn't buy anything. As the road pitched downward they began to see the giant bones of skeletons protruding from the pit's walls, the remains of huge creatures that hadn't been excavated.

The road opened into a large square, were a hundred people or so bustled about a series of tables, trading wares for food and coin. The square was surrounded by four massive skeletons, all of which had signs hanging out front that read: vacancy. Above, Sayzar could see the blue sky and white clouds as they floated by.

The main portion of each skeleton looked like a large clear dome supported by white curved ceiling joists, with tunnels and fissures leading to other chambers in the beast's skull, arms, and legs, of which the creatures appeared to have had many. Most were lit by oil lamps made of bone, and blackened from years of use. Copper piping ran this way and that, attached to the bone with silver ties. At the end of each pipe there was a funnel, and the twisted old system provided instant communication throughout Bonetown.

When Sayzar saw the sign for The Bonemarrow Inn, he knew they'd found their place. They entered through two swinging doors that were made of bone and decorated with an intricate pattern of flowers, and above the flowers tiny lights depicted the starwisps as they darted about in their uncoordinated dance. The main room in the ribcage consisted of tables and a long bar. A staircase made from one of the dead creature's giant paws led up into a series of guestrooms carved in the skeleton's backbone, each vertebra a private quarters. They grabbed a table, its smooth white surface stained red with wine.

"Newbies, huh? What can I get you?" said a waitress, her hair held in place by a series of bone fragments.

"That obvious, huh?" said Sayzar.

"Not many people live here, mister?"

"Sayzar."

"The traders we mostly know, so it's rare to see

a newbie. You here for moonglow?"

"And the starwisps," said Taeda, and Sayzar wished she hadn't.

"Wine all around, please," said Sayzar, dismissing the women before anyone else said something stupid. "Oh," said Sayzar, as he grabbed the women's shirtsleeve. "We'll need a few rooms also."

"I'll send Graj over," she said.

When she was gone, Sayzar barked, "Will you shut up! You think we're the only ones here to try and read the prophesy during moonglow?" *But we are the only ones who have Taeda*, he thought.

They were on their third carafe of wine when Graj made his appearance. A short man with hair all over his head, face, and visible body parts, he had the presence of a desert rat. "I only have two rooms. How long you need?"

"Three nights," said Sayzar.

"Yeah, like everyone else. Moonglow. The three most expensive nights in the hotel's history. It will cost you ten gold."

"Ten gold!" blurted Damroth, and Sayzar shot him a dirty look.

"Five," said Sayzar, who had financed the entire mission, from the balloons, to their supplies and weapons. But he was running out of coin, and if there were any major expenses beyond this one, there would be trouble.

* * *

The first night of moonglow was total chaos. As daylight faded, and the three large moons floated in the sky, a gray haze settled over Bonetown and the surrounding area. At midnight folks began experiencing magic. Some people flew about, moved large objects with their minds, and displayed a variety of other talents.

Some believed that moonglow was a test created by the starwisps to see what they would do, or would have done, had they been given starwisp magic. If that were the case, many of the inhabitants of Bonetown would have failed.

As the moonglow festival raged, fights broke out, and there was some looting. Graj locked down The Bonemarrow Inn, and the party had hunkered down in their rooms, watching the chaos through open windows, and listening to the hollering and screaming echo through the old bones. Pathina had quietly left the group with Sayzar's permission so she could see if her talent worked, and it had. Like her relatives from the distant past, Pathina could read minds during moonglow, and so it was that she was

able to warn Sayzar of the coming attack.

She'd been on her way back, when she saw a group of men standing in the passageway by one of their rooms. She paused, closing her eyes and picturing the scene in her head, when the images rocked her backward, and she almost fell back down the bone steps the way she had come.

She raced forward, pushing past the men and entering Sayzar's room, and so was able to help them lock things down before the men had a chance to attack. They had pounded on the bone door for several minutes, one of them trying to use his moonglow magical strength to break the door down, but the old bone had held, and the men had given up.

The second night of moonglow was much worse. They had decided to take a walk around, see what was happening, and Pam had been killed in a knife fight. Krispin fled, and they hadn't seen him since. After that Sayzar decided they should stay in their rooms as much as possible until the final night of moonglow, the night the starwisps were supposed to come.

4

Even though Taeda had seen a detailed sketch of the ruins that Sayzar thought told of the location of Izril's flute, Sayzar wanted to scout the location beforehand anyway, just to make sure there were no surprises. The starwisps would overlap with the moonglow for one night, and it wouldn't happen again for ten thousand cycles. They had one chance, and tonight was it.

The ancient language was carved into a huge breastplate deep within Bonetown. The deeper you went into the ancient graveyard the less populated things became. There was no counting how many of the giant beasts had come to die there, but if the partial skeletons they saw were any indication, the count was in the thousands. Sayzar paused when he came to a large carved archway that led away into darkness.

He paused, turning to look at Damroth, Pathina, and Taeda, who followed behind, eyes wide, and weapons at the ready. The arch had been carved through solid bone, and music notes with faces in various states of repose decorated it, some wearing expressions of joy, some horror. Sayzar removed a cylinder from his pack and clicked it open, revealing a thin piece of metal at its top. He began twisting a lever, which spun a piece of fine metal inside the cylinder causing heat, and igniting the filament at the top of the tube creating a bright light.

"Stay close," said Sayzar, as he entered the

gaping maw of bone.

They hadn't gone far when they reached the section of bone with the saying on it. Two people were also there, a woman with long dark blonde hair, and a man wearing a hood. The man with the hood fled when they arrived, and Sayzar caught sight of blonde hair and blue eyes as the person rushed by, and for an instant he thought of Krispin.

The women eyed them briefly, and then went back to sketching the wall. The great breastplate was cracked in several spots, but the symbols etched therein were still easy to see. Over the years vandals had tried to cut out pieces of the wall, and some had been successful, but the missing pieces left no real mystery as to what had been there, and it didn't take much skill to recreate the missing pieces in one's mind.

Damroth looked at Sayzar, and said, "I'll be able to cover the entrance while you do your thing tonight, but will you be able to handle the people that will be in here? The chamber holds twenty or thirty," he said, looking around.

"I'll have to," said Sayzar. "Taeda will be working and writing, and Pathina can read some minds, see what the folks around us are thinking. That should at least give us a head start if things go bad." Damroth nodded. Plan formulated, location scouted, the four of them headed back to the Bonemarrow, had a few drinks and some food, and went to rest. The starwisps would be here in a few short hours, and they'd be ready.

* * *

They weren't ready. They had all overslept, the sun long gone; when Taeda woke in a panic, sweat dripping down her face. Sayzar laughed, and told everyone to calm down. It was best that they wait until right before the starwisps died out, let things calm down a bit, let the night run its course, before they went. He made them wait two nervous hours, as they watched the starwisps dive and jump across the sky, before they gathered their belongings, and left their rooms at The Bonemarrow Inn for the last time. If things went as planned, they'd leave town tonight while everyone was sleeping off their wine.

They arrived at the wall in the dead of night, and there were only a few people there. If there had been a large crowd prior, they were gone now. They couldn't see the starwisps from so deep inside Bonetown, but Taeda could feel them. She had tested her magic on an ancient tomb that she had been translating for many cycles, and she had found that her vision blurred as the magic took over her body,

and she felt the meaning of the words. She also felt pretty sure that there was something new in her, the moonglow extending her power, but she had no idea what the additional magic could do.

As Taeda started reading the symbols carved into the great wall of bone, she immediately began showing signs of the Hoad, the transformation of the starwisps. The Hoad only happened the first time one felt the starwisp magic, but with the moonglow in play, no one knew what to expect.

Taeda fell to her knees, and two people nearby turned to watch. Pathina closed her eyes, reading their minds, but the people meant them no ill will. Yet. Taeda was rocking back and forth, her head in her hands. Periodically, she would look up, stare blankly at the symbols etched into the slab of bone, and then turn her head, screaming.

They had a small crowd around them now, and Damroth had pulled his sword. "Those two men in the back are thinking about taking over the situation," said Pathina, and Sayzar directed Damroth toward them, putting himself between them and Taeda.

The unseen starwisps above blinked out, and the moonglow's gray shadow began to brighten. Taeda screamed, and fell forward into Sayzar's waiting grasp. "I've got it. Let's go," said Taeda, and Sayzar helped her to her feet, and the party left the chamber.

Once they had found a quiet area inside a skull of one of the ancient beasts, Sayzar opened his copy of the prophesy, and spread it out before Taeda. She looked at it for several more moments before she spoke. "This is a warning not to disturb the flute, and below is series of warnings for anyone who attempts to retrieve the flute. The creator wanted…

"Yes, yes, yes," spat Sayzar. "But is the location there?"

"Starless Tangle," said Taeda, and silence fell. The Starless Tangle was an area to the south in Tanglewood forest. It was said to be a place of great evil.

Sayzar smiled. Now that he had the location, the power in the group shifted from Taeda to him. With the starwisps gone, and the moonglow fading, Pathina and Taeda were of no use to him any longer. Then he thought of something he hadn't before. They were only useless to him until he found the flute.

5

The landscape was strange and new. A dark blue sky lit by the ancient sun filled the horizon. Sayzar stood in a meadow, tall gloomy trees all around him. The trees were huge, bigger than anything Sayzar or anyone in his party had ever seen. Though they had seen glimpses of the trees as they flew over the eastern edge of the forest in their balloons, that experience hadn't prepared them the immensity of the trees.

Everyone in the party had heard of Starless Tangle, a legendary swamp hole in the northeast portion of Tanglewood Forest. Sayzar had seen it once, from a distance. It was nothing more than a black smudge on the world at night, and a bright window into nothingness during the day. What the area was, or what lived there, Sayzar didn't know. He had no idea how he was going to get into the tangle, and what he would do when he did.

Further examination of the prophecy had revealed nothing of use. There were no specifics at all other than the location of the flute, and Damroth had suggested that they abandon the quest and head to Dusktown, which lay in the center of the forest. Then they could wait until the next starwisp cycle, and maybe bring magic with them.

Sayzar had rejected the idea. He felt the more people who knew about the flute and its whereabouts, the hairier things would get for them. Taeda and Pathina agreed with Sayzar, not that it mattered. Sayzar was the only one who knew how to get to Starless Tangle, and he wouldn't go there until he was good and ready.

They left the clearing and plunged into the thick woods, where the air got cool and stagnant. Pathina hadn't been much help so far, but Sayzar realized the potential of having her with him at all times once he had the flute. He would be able to read the mind of any person at any time. He didn't know for sure if the flute would give magic to people who had never experienced starwisp magic and only the moonglow, but the ancient legends he had heard said it did.

They walked most of the day, stopping only once under a huge tree to eat, and have some wine. "We'll be there by tonight. An ideas how to proceed?" asked Sayzar. All three of them had good reason to help Sayzar still, and it was more than just the money he had promised them. If Sayzar did get his hands on the flute, and it worked, he would be a very rich and powerful man.

"You say it's just a black patch? Nothing else visible?"" asked Damroth.

"Yep. Looks like a dark patch of sky with no stars," said Sayzar.

"Hence the name Starless Tangle," said Pathina.

"So we just walk in?" asked Sayzar.

"That's what I was thinking. Maybe leave one person behind to watch our backs?" said Taeda, and Sayzar nodded. They were a good team, and suddenly his thoughts of dumping them seemed foolish.

They broke free of the trees sooner than Sayzar had predicted. The sun had just dropped, and dusk lay like a blanket over the forest. In the distance a black smudge hovered above the ground—no grass, no trees, no underbrush, nothing but black nothingness that looked like a giant bruise on the face of the world.

"This is it," said Sayzar. "Pathina, can you stay?" Sayzar's purpose for leaving Pathina behind was cold and calculated. He might need Damroth for his muscle, and going forward Pathina would be more valuable than Taeda once he had the flute.

"Fine," she said, sitting down, and staring into the woods. "Call if you need me."

Since they had no idea what to expect, they had nothing to plan for, so they just dove in. "Stay with me," said Sayzar, as he plunged into the inky darkness.

6

The darkness was even more complete than Sayzar thought possible.

Within the Starless Tangle the light of dusk disappeared and they stood in total and impenetrable blackness. They couldn't see their hands in front of their faces, nor the ground beneath their feet. They just stood there for a few moments, unable to tell what direction they were facing, or in what direction they should precede.

"You see that?" asked Taeda, but in the darkness neither he nor Damroth saw where she was pointing. Sayzar jumped when he felt Taeda's hand on his arm, as she raised it and guided his gaze toward a pinprick of light in the distance.

"I see it now," said Damroth.

"Grab the back of my pants, Damroth, and Taeda grab onto Damroth's. Stay with me," said Sayzar, as he started forward, taking several uncomfortable steps, the ground nothing but a black maw beneath his feet.

They walked on, though in truth none of them knew how far or long they walked. Slowly, the light began to grow, but when it seemed like they had walked for hours, Taeda asked, "Can we rest for a bit?" The three of them sat huddled in the darkness as they consumed some water and a few pieces of bread.

Once they were on the move again, Taeda said, "Do you think we're doing something wrong? At this rate it will take weeks to get to the light."

It didn't take weeks, but they were bone weary and starving when the dot of light disappeared and they were in the clearing again, under a cover of thick darkness. The nothingness was gone, but all the trees and plants around the clearing seemed to have eyes, and their gaze followed the party's every move. When Sayzar looked back, he could see Pathina standing by the edge of the forest, her keen eyes starring past them. They had only moved fifty feet.

"Look!" shouted Taeda, her voice loud in the silent forest.

A man sat a few feet away, whittling on something, and humming a tune Sayzar knew well. As they watched, it became clear to Sayzar and his friends that the man wasn't real. The coloring of his face and clothes were sharp enough, but his body had no depth. It was like he was a colored shadow.

"I assume since you are standing before me that you have discovered the fate of my world, and all the clues that led you to search for my flute," said the old man, his voice peaceful.

Sayzar had surmised from the prophecy, as well as the prophecy's location, that the flute had been carved from a bone that had come from the beast whose skeleton had been inscribed with the location of the flute. Apparently, they had skipped a few steps, and it appeared that the ancients hadn't been aware of moonglow.

The man said, "I was starting to think, as my chronometer ticked on, that maybe the planet had changed too much, burying my clues too deep." The man went back to whittling, paying Sayzar and his companions no mind.

Sayzar looked at Taeda and Damroth, both of whom shrugged. So they waited as the old man carved, and only one moon floated overhead. The three moons wouldn't appear together again for a thousand cycles. Hours passed, and finally the man put down his knife, and blew tentatively into the flute he had just created.

The instrument was beautiful to behold. Made of bone, with flower and vine accents carved into every inch of its length, and it seemed to glow in the pale darkness.

Sayzar was on his feet, staring at the flute like a child stared at ice cream. He took several steps forward, stopped, looked back at Taeda and Damroth, and then watched the old man who was looking Sayzar up and down, like he was a piece of meat the old man was considering buying.

"You want my flute?" asked the old man. Sayzar nodded his head yes. "And what will you do with it, may I ask?"

Sayzar thought this type of test might happen, so he had thought long about why exactly he wanted the flute. Clearly riches and fame weren't the right answer, though that was why he had started his quest. But now, standing in the Starless Tangle, the darkness pressing in around him, he thought of other things. Helping people, making the world a better place. And who said he couldn't get rich doing that?

"I want to play for the people," said Sayzar. "To help the world and make it a better place to live."

This seemed to please the old man, and he smiled. "I have no way of knowing if your intentions are true, of course, since I am nothing but a hologram from the distant past, but there will be no test. No challenges or tasks you must complete. You have followed the clues across the seas of time and you will be rewarded. Use it well," said the old man, and the flute appeared in Sayzar's hand.

The cool bone felt good, and he turned to look at his companions who were filled with a joy he hadn't seen in them before. Taeda stepped forward, her book of ancient writings in her hands. Then Sayzar had a momentary flash of panic. He didn't know how to play the flute.

The panic subsided, however, as he blew several squeaky notes, but in moments he was playing a basic scale as his fingers flowed easily up and down the flute. Taeda stared at her book. Nothing. She looked up at Sayzar with worried eyes, than back at Damroth, but as Sayzar continued to play the jumble of symbols on the page transformed, like they did when the starwisps came, and she could read the text.

Taeda burst out in laughter, and Sayzar continued to play, the notes uncoordinated, but pleasant. As he played, daylight pierced the dark nothingness of Starless Tangle, and the shadows burnt away like dew under the sun's harsh morning light. Sayzar played, his childlike music odd, but endearing.

As the notes from Izril's flute carried on the breeze, Starless Tangle dissipated, then blew away, and was gone from the world. With it had gone the old man, and Sayzar, Taeda, and Damroth stood alone in the small clearing. Pathina stood watching them, smiling from the edge of the forest.

Sayzar looked to Pathina, then began playing the flute the best he could, watching to see the expression on her face. "Pure joy!" she yelled. "You are thinking about pure joy!" Her moonglow magic worked. The flute was what the fables had said it was.

When finally they looked for the old man, they found that he was gone, and all he had left behind was an odd looking structure made of a metal none of them had ever seen before. They entered the capsule, and found a series of lights, buttons, and flat pieces of glass that showed moving pictures from all around the world.

Sayzar knew then that he and his friends had been called to do more than just use their magic to get rich, and he realized that what he had told the old man was true. There would always be time to get rich, but now all he could think about was the ancient people that used to inhabit his world, where they had gone, and why.

Sunlight steamed through the trees, and Sayzar relaxed. Things hadn't turned out the way he had planned, but did they ever? As he and he companions planned their next move, the sun rose high over the land, warming their skin, and their hearts.

Unknown to Our Maps

There are places
Unknown to our maps,
Uncaught by cartographers,
Uncharted by those arted
In drawing longitudes,
Those with attitudes
For scribing latitudes.
And there be found
Dinosaurs alive,
And unicorns and dragons,
Giants and pixies both,
And all of faerie,
And all of legend,
And all of myth,
And all of tale
Rhymed and sung,
For those who desire
To be so mapless
Will not be confirmed
Inside a dusty atlas.

— K.S. Hardy

Talisman Book Reviews

Tarnish
J.D. Brink
Fugitive Fiction
$15.99, Trade Paperback
400 pages

Tarnish, by J.D. Brink, is a novel about the power of storytelling—the influence of myth versus truth. Billy Cole has grown up under the influence of the heroic tales of the Colors Three—rather like a fantastic version of the Three Musketeers. Billy's aging father, Ian the Black, and Billy's mentor, Trevor the Red, are all that's left of the once glorious trio, now long retired from adventuring. The tales of their epic battles and valiant deeds inspire Billy to undertake his own quest. When his hometown falls under the attack of a mysterious, malevolent force, Billy sets out alone to recruit a band of champions to fight on behalf of his village.

On the road, Billy renames himself William Thunderstrike and earns his room and board at various inns and taverns by telling stories about The Colors Three. But he learns from his audiences that every story has two sides, truth is usually influenced by perspective, and the reality of a warrior's life is more often brutal more than glorious. Along with the greater plot, Brink illustrates the theme through a series of stories-within-the-story, and his imagination for crafting heroic folk tales is unbelievably prolific.

The strength of *Tarnish* is Billy's coming-of-age narrative, his quest to develop his own, innate heroism, and his struggle to reconcile illustrious legends with harsher truths. Billy falls in with a band of men led by Leon Shimmerskin, a neo-myth in the making. Billy hopes Shimmerskin will be the savior of his village, but the more time Billy spends with Shimmerskin the more Billy learns about the differences between noble champion and self-serving mercenary. After engaging in several violent capers with Shimmerskin's gang, Billy questions who he is becoming and whether it is the kind of man he really wants to be.

Tarnish's settings are well established and distinct. Its characters are richly drawn. Brink makes a deliberate effort to give his heroes realistic flaws rather than making them omnipotent, infallible "stone asses" (as Billy calls them). If *Tarnish* has a weakness, then it is its pacing. Brink is no slacker when it comes to world building, but the establishment of this complex character history relies on the myriad folk tales told throughout the novel, and I felt they had a tendency to slow the pacing, particularly in the places where Billy recounted multiple legends in one sitting.

Because of some mild sexual content and violence, *Tarnish* is probably most appropriate for older teens and adults. And because the female characters are mostly foils or accessories for the male characters, this story will probably appeal more to men. *Tarnish's* high fantasy styling is tempered by comfortable, somewhat modern language, a relatable, every-man main character, and a universal theme that transcends the genre.

— Karissa B. Sluss

Solomon the Peacemaker
Hunter Welles
Cowcatcher Press
$16.00, Trade Paperback
227 pages

For this first novel, Hunter Welles has come up with an unusual narrative device—the story is told in the form of an interview with a suspected terrorist, Vincent Alan Chell, but only Chell's half of the interview is given. The interrogator's name and remarks are not recorded here to avoid putting his life in jeopardy, so we only get Chell's side of things. Alas, Welles doesn't do much with this approach and there is little to suggest the "face officer's" point of view.

Chell speaks early on about his wife Yael's suicide, then spells out in detail their life in a future world divided between those living inside node cities such as Boston and the Siders who live outside the nodes. We don't learn much about the anarchistic Siders because Chell remains in the node world which is dominated by Solomon the Peacemaker. Solomon is a super computer that runs the node cities and for most of the story is referred to simply as the Peacemaker.

For reasons not made completely clear, the Peacemaker needs to have a human host plugged into it and this feature becomes the focus of attack by those opposed to the ruling machine. The host only lasts seven years before a new one is recruited to replace it. Chell and Yael join a group plotting against the Peacemaker—Yael devoted to the effort, Chell only lukewarm at first. Led by a cult figure called the Preacher, there is an aborted attack, leading to Yael's suicide. Chell takes a second wife, also opposed to the Peacemaker, and eventually they devise a plan using the host against Solomon.

This novel is easy reading, with believable and interesting characters and an intriguing if sparsely developed future society. What it lacks is a believable villain. With the interrogator silent and the actual "crimes" of the Peacemaker and its handlers left to the imagination, it's hard to get really disturbed by the computer and its host. I wouldn't want to live in the Peacemaker's world either, but I'd need a lot more convincing before I tried to bring it down.

And why does all this take place a hundred and seventy years in the future? Seems to me Solomon is almost here.

— Neal Wilgus

The Raven's Warrior
Vincent Pratchett
YMAA Publications Center, Inc.
$14.95, Trade Paperback
335 pages

This is Vincent Pratchett's first novel and it's obviously intended as an epic that incorporates, if not Everything, then a Hell of a Lot. The story takes place around 900 AD and follows the adventures of a Celtic warrior, first known as Victor, who is enslaved by the Vikings and taken to the Mid-East, then through the desert to the "Middle Kingdom" of China. There he

is freed and taken as an apprentice by a warrior priest named Mah Lin and his daughter Selah. Victor is re-named Arkthar and it's no spoiler when I mention that Mah Lin is also called Merlin, his daughter Sea Lass.

Under the guidance of Mah Lin and Selah, Arkthar learns to read and write and masters meditation, philosophy, science, medicine, the martial arts, and steel weapon making—all preparations for the battle to come. Those battles are mostly against the Supreme Commander, Mah Lin's life-long foe and bad guy of the epic. Our heroes are accompanied by Selah's mysterious raven and later by a beggar who appears to be Death, even though he helps stop the small pox epidemic the Commander has loosened on the land. In the final confrontation, Arkthar even manages to invent the very first pressure cooker bomb.

There's a lot to like in this story, but it seems more like a first draft than a finished product. I'm not sympathetic to editorial meddling, but I can't help thinking Pratchett could have used some advice about overwriting, confusing points of view, and irritating little things like names. The Supreme Commander, for instance, has no name, nor does the raven, for that matter. The Commander's page, who becomes an important character toward the end, is simply called the page. The crone is just the crone. The rebel is the rebel. Even the Emperor of China is merely the emperor. Maybe that's why they're all stick figures. The book is also in need of better proofreading.

Vincent Pratchett is originally from the United Kingdom and presently lives in Toronto, Canada. He is a cousin of British science fiction/fantasy writer Terry Pratchett, and is a world traveler, martial artist, and professional firefighter. *The Raven's Warrior* ends with enough loose ends that a sequel seems likely. Stay tuned.

— Neal Wilgus

About the talisman scale:
Books are ranked on a scale of five talismans with five being the most recommended and one being the least.

If you would like a book reviewed:
Please drop a note to David Lee Summers at hadrosaur@zianet.com and he will help you get your book to one of our reviewers.

Grim Series
Kristine Ong Muslim
Popcorn Press
$9.95, Trade Paperback
114 Pages

In Grim Series, Kristine Ong Muslim treats us to eighty-seven deliciously dark poems. The book is divided into six sections which, at first, appear unrelated, but soon are woven into an interesting thematic continuity exploring our relationships with our own bodies, our families, our neighbors, and those cosmic forces which seem beyond our control.

The first section is entitled "Conrad". These eight poems present snapshots of a constructed boy and the family who loves him. Throughout this section, Muslim shows us that Conrad is both frightening and divine through a series of lines that recur in several of the poems:

> We were all yellow inside,
> The wrong shade of yellow—
> The color of the gods.

The second section is entitled "Giger's Tracts". The title evokes the artwork of H.R. Giger who passed away earlier this year. These poems take the form of tourist tracts through grisly landscapes, not unlike those envisioned by Giger, ranging from our own insides, to the apocalypse, and into hyperspace. In "The Invisible Tourists", Muslim suggests a reason for taking such a tour:

> to make us remember
> to make us understand
> we are so much
> like them inside.

Part three is entitled "Muir's Horses" and each poem is a meditation on Edwin Muir's 1960 poem, "The Horses." The original is a look at war and the peace that follows. Muslim suggests that the peace following war is death. This is exemplified in the poem "After the Arrival of the Strange Horses."

> Only the dead have enough
> surplus energy to ride them.

In the section entitled "Vengeful Villagers," Muslim presents us with a series of character sketches. We meet children tossed down a well, plotting revenge against their father. A woman transforms those who wronged her into strange creatures inhabiting an aquarium tank. A girl evokes horrific reactions from her dolls by telling them stories. Ghosts wait to pounce on a couple looking at a new house. Perhaps this section is best summed up in this couplet from the poem "Tonight":

> Worms slithered within the hollows of my eyes,
> wanting to see my visions.

The section titled "Body Horror" is not as cringe-inducing as one might at first think. Although the section includes images of pins in eyes and ribs bursting through chests, it seems more concerned with the horror of being a spirit trapped within a body. This is encapsulated in the poem "Hunger" where Muslim writes:

> Blunt as it may sound,
> we are moved by hunger first.
> Our hunger makes us who we are.

The book concludes with a section entitled "Strangers" and chronicles sixteen different traveling salesmen, messiahs, victims, and lovers. Perhaps they're all aspects of the same being. In either case, the final poem, "The Last Stranger" brings together elements of all the previous sections and serves as a summary to the entire collection. In the end, *Grim Series* reminds me of the cartoons of Charles Addams or the Elliot Family stories of Ray Bradbury. They use the darkness to reveal something about ourselves. Whereas Addams and Bradbury focused on family, Muslim extends her vision to a whole village—a village well worth visiting if you're a fan of dark poetry.

— David Lee Summers

From Space
Cardinal Cox
Starburker Publications
$2.00 Suggested, Chapbook
Email: cardinalcox1@yahoo.co.uk
16 pages

This leaflet of poems was inspired by the Space Fact and Fiction Exhibit held at the Peterborough Museum in the UK in October 2013. There are thirteen poems here, ranging from "Some People Call It Culture" (dedicated to the late SF fan Iain Banks) and "Orbital Observatory" (celebrating Sir Fred Hoyle) to "Hard Work on the Red Shift" (for astroartist Chris Wakelin) and "Drone Strike" (credited to Chin at the Stamford Pint of Poetry group). Cox concludes with the libertarian "Liberty Stars" and a rousing "Film on the Evening News." As he does with all his leaflets, Cox includes a brief commentary at the end of each poem.

Cardinal Cox was appointed Poet Laureate of Peterborough in 2003 and has won numerous awards for his work including the annual Data Dump Award for best SF/F poetry published in the UK. He read his poems at the 2013 World Fantasy Convention in Brighton, as well as at steampunk events and at the We Love Words festival and elsewhere. He self-publishes several leaflets of verse each year, most of it in the realm of SF/F/H, with a side series devoted to the Cthulhu Mythos and another to the King in Yellow.

Cox is a lively spirit well worth checking into. Recommended.

— Neal Wilgus

About the Contributors

Currently hard at work on a novel, **Steven J. Bitz** has had three other pieces published in various magazines. Much like a certain spy takes his martini and a zombie prefers his brains, the author's ideas are shaken, not stirred.

Simon Bleaken is a long-time fan of the Sci-fi, fantasy and horror genres. His fiction has appeared in several magazines and chapbooks, including: *Lovecraft's Disciples, Strange Sorcery, Night Land, Beneath the Moons of Zandor, Weird World of Zandor* as well as in previous issues of *Tales of the Talisman*. He has also appeared in the anthologies: *Eldritch Horrors: Dark Tales* and *Space Horrors: Full-Throttle Space Tales #4*. He was also the winner of the first-ever short story competition held by the Museum of Witchcraft in Boscastle, Cornwall. He is a supporter of Greenpeace, the World Wildlife Fund and the Stonewall charity, as well as a member of OBOD and British Mensa. He lives near Bristol, England.

Mark Anthony Brennan lives off the west coast of Canada on Vancouver Island. He is a member of SFWA and SFCanada, with numerous publishing credits to his name. In addition to pursuing his master's degree at the University of Victoria, he is also a music critic and journalist.

Kelda Crich is a new born entity. She's been lurking in her creator's mind for a few years. Now she's out in the open. Find her in London looking at strange things in medical museums or on her blog. Her poems have appeared in *Nameless, Cthulhu Haiku II* and the *Future Lovecraft* anthology.

Douglas Empringham has had fiction accepted by *Black Gate, Space and Time, The Lamp-Post, Leading Edge, The Armchair Aesthete, Rosebud* and other genre and literary magazines including both *Tales of the Talisman* and *Hadrosaur Tales*.

A frequent contributor to both *Tales of the Talisman* and *Hadrosaur Tales*, **Gary Every** is the author of the science fiction novella *The Saint and the Robot*, which is based upon a medieval legend concerning the youth of Thomas Aquinas. *Shadow of the OhshaD*, a collection of the best of his award winning newspaper columns about Arizona's Native Americans, history, and environment is also available at Amazon.com or his website www.garyevery.com

Wayne Faust has been a full time music and comedy performer for over 35 years (www.waynefaust.com). While on the road he writes fiction, mostly of the speculative variety. Since he has been writing songs from an early age, he learned to say everything he needed to say in three verses or less, so his prose tends to be tightly-written and fast moving. He is happy to have yet another story included in an edition of *Tales of the Talisman*.

As a child, **Kathy Ferrell** refused to share her crayons, preferring to eat them all herself. Today she is an artist and writer working from her decidedly sinister 19th century home, nestled deep in the backwoods of Appalachia. When not creating, she can be found wrapped in a shawl, drinking tea and wondering what on earth could be making that incessant creaking on the stair. She also uses the internet, in spite of being warned.
　Paintings: cuposwank.carbonmade.com
　Words: cuposwank.wordpress.com

Neil T. Foster is a freelance artist who lives in Australia. He has penciled and inked various comic books, recently completing an online comic—*Beware the Beast*—for the official International Planet of the Apes Fan Club. He has done illustrations and painted covers for various SF fanzines, CD booklets and computer games. His work includes everything from illustration, cartoons, logos and comic strips to artwork for action figure packaging. His illustrations and painting have also appeared in *The Corpse* and *Black Petals* Magazines.

Laura Givens is a Denver-based author and artist. Her art has graced the covers of numerous publishers' books and magazines. She has provided illustrations for *Orson Scott Card's Intergalactic Medicine Show, Jim Baen's Universe, Talebones, Science Fiction Trails* and *Tales of the Talisman*. Her work may be viewed at www.lauragivens-artist.com. In 2010 she naively decided she could probably write stories as good as many she had illustrated. She has sold works ranging from zombie stories to space operas. She was co-editor and contributor to *Six-Guns Straight From*

Hell, a weird western anthology, and is art director for *Tales of the Talisman* magazine.

Morland Gonsoulin is a traditionally trained artist and avid science fiction fan living in Colorado Springs, Colorado. He has done artwork for various publications before, including *Tales of the Talisman* Magazine.

K.S. Hardy has had fantasy poetry appear in many publications over the years including *Dreamscapes and Nightmares*, *Not One of Us*, *Mythic Delirium*, and more. His short stories have been featured in *Tales of the Talisman*, *Beyond Centauri*, and *Lore* (drawing comment from Brian Lumly). He has been nominated for a Rhysling Award. And his first children's book, *Her Best Trick or Treat, Ever* with a safe, scary theme has just come out, signed copies are exclusively available through Library House Children's Books, Grand Rapids, OH 43522.

C.J. Henderson is the creator of the Piers Knight supernatural investigator series and the Teddy London occult detective series. With seventy books and/or novels to his credit, along with hundreds and hundreds of short stories and comics as well as thousands of non-fiction pieces in print, he is one of the hardest working authors to not only survive half of the last century but to be able to continue onward into this one no matter how horrid and bleak it might appear. For more information on this truly unique individual, to read more of his fiction for free, or to simply comment on his story in this volume, please feel free to drop in on him at www.cjhenderson.com. Tell him *Talisman* sent you.

Jack Herbert is a mystery and science fiction writer as well as an award-winning game designer. His work has appeared in several print and on-line magazines including *Step'Cross* and *The Current*. He currently resides in Chicago.

Tom Kelly received a degree in Graphic Design from Lycoming College and holds a master's degree in Sequential Art from the Savannah College of Art and Design. Tom has worked for several years producing graphic design and illustration for numerous design and production companies. As a freelance artist, Tom has produced illustrations and cartoons using a wide variety of classical and electronic techniques. Tom focuses on creating dynamic visuals by fusing together a wide variety of elements into one thought-provoking illustration. Tom's sequential work focuses on the power of bold black and white elements as well as the power of graphic design to relate a narrative.

Edward J. McFadden III juggles a full-time career as a university administrator and teacher, with his writing aspirations. His first novel, a mysterious dark-thriller called *The Black Death of Babylon,* is now available from Post Mortem Press. His steampunk fantasy novelette, *Starwisps,* was recently published in the anthology *Fantastic Stories of the Imagination,* and his novella *Anywhere But Here* is available from Padwolf Publishing. He is the author/editor of six published books: *Jigsaw Nation, Deconstructing Tolkien: A Fundamental Analysis of The Lord of the Rings* (to be re-released in eBook format Fall 2012), *Time Capsule, The Second Coming, Thoughts of Christmas,* and *The Best of Pirate Writings.* He has had more than 50 short stories published in places like *Fantastic Futures 13, From Beyond the Grave, Apocalypse 13, Hear Them Roar, CrimeSpree Magazine,Terminal Fright, Cyber-Psycho's AOD, The And,* and *The Arizona Literary Review.* Over the last seven years he has written six novels, all of which are at various stages of rewriting and submission for publication. He lives on Long Island with his wife Dawn, their daughter Samantha, and their mutt Oli. See EdwardMcfadden.com for all things Ed.

Erika McGinnis has been painting and drawing since she was very young. She earned her Bachelor of Fine Arts from Boise State University (go Broncos!) in 1998 with an emphasis in art history. Erika is a member of the International Association of Astronomical Artists (www.IAAA.org) and is an avid science fiction reader, from where a lot of her inspiration comes. Her art has shown at various scifi conventions around the country and has won "Best of Show" quite a few times. Erika instructs watercolor classes for the Idaho Academy of fine Arts and youth art through Young Rembrandts. She has done numerous illustrations for books, CD covers and magazines, such as *Farscape - Season Three, With Friends Like These,* and *Tales of the Talisman.* Her *New Star Tarot Deck* and *Boxed Set* are available through Barnes and Noble and various online booksellers.

Erika owns a company called *Under the Cobalt Sky, Llc.,* which carries a line of products featuring her artwork for yoga wear with proceeds benefiting the Humane Society and jewelry that emphasizes the different ages of art history. These are available at museum shops and online on her website: www.erikamcginnis.com.

Erika lives in Boise, ID, with her husband, jazz saxophonist Sandon Mayhew and their dog, Thelonious.

F.T. McKinstry is the author of the *Chronicles of Eal-iron,* a fantasy series by Double Dragon Publishing. Her short stories appear in *Tales of the Talisman, Aiofe's Kiss,* and *Wizards, Woods and Gods: Tales of Integration,* Wild Child Publishing. When she's not writing or reading weird things, she's hanging out with her cats and fishes, tinkering in gardens, shoveling snow or smearing paint on canvases. Find out more at ftmckinstry.com.

Lance J. Mushung graduated from the Georgia Institute of Technology with an aerospace engineering degree. He worked for over 30 years with NASA contractors in Houston, Texas performing engineering work on the Space Shuttle and its payloads. Now retired, he writes science fiction.

Paul Niemiec plays guitar in a swing band—atomic pablo. Check it out at myspace.com. Paul's first job in high school was an art job doing safety filmstrips for hard-rock miners. After that, the office situation—smooth jazz radio, and chain-smoking co-workers—really put him off commercial art.

After a long hiatus, he got back into drawing. Paul was trying to figure out which way a camel's front legs bent, and he decided to go to the zoo to draw camels. Later, he met some of the Squid Works guys at a figure drawing class.

Robert E. Porter has gone to ground somewhere in the Midwest with his cat, his laptop, and a library card. His nonfiction credits include "Some Hope For Us All" in *Scifaikuest.*

James Frederick William Rowe is a young and up and coming author and poet out of Brooklyn, New York, with works appearing in *Heroic Fantasy Quarterly, Big Pulp,* and *Andromeda Spaceways Inflight Magazine.* When not writing fantasy, science fiction, and horror fiction and poetry, he is pursuing a Ph.D. in philosophy and works in a variety of freelance positions. The poet's website can be found at http://jamesfwrowe.wordpress.com

Noel Sloboda is the author of the poetry collections *Shell Games* (2008) and *Our Rarer Monsters* (2013) as well as several chapbooks. He has also published a book about Edith Wharton and Gertrude Stein. Sloboda surves as dramturg for the Harrisburg Shakespeare Company and teaches at Penn State York.

Jason Sturner grew up along the Fox River in northern Illinois. Of his many jobs, those he most enjoyed were naturalist and botanist. His stories and poems have appeared in *Space and Time Magazine, Star*Line, Tales of the Talisman, Morpheus Tales,* and *Liquid Imagination,* among others. He currently lives in Knoxville, Tennessee, near the Great Smoky Mountains. Website: www.jasonsturner.blogsopot.com.

Anna Sykora has been an attorney in New York and teacher of English in Germany, where she resides with her patient husband and three enormous cats. She has placed hundreds of stories and poems, mostly genre, in the small press, and lately made the finals of *Rosebud* magazine's Mary Shelley SF competition. Motto: eat your rejections like pretzels; they cannot make you fat.

With over a million words in print **Patrick Thomas** keeps busy writing the fantasy humor series *Murphy's Lore* (*Tales From Bulfinche's Pub, Fools' Day, Through the Drinking Glass, Shadow of the Wolf, Redemption Road, Bartender of the Gods, Nightcaps* and *Empty Graves*) as well as the *After Hours* spin offs *Fairy With A Gun, Fairy Rides the Lightning, Dead To Rites, Rites of Passage,* and *Lore & Dysorder.* His Mystic Investigators paranormal mystery series has grown to include *Bullets & Brimstone* and *From The Shadows*—both with John L. French; and *Once More Upon A Time* and the upcoming *Partners In Crime*—both with Diane Raetz. He co-edited *New Blood* and *Hear Them Roar.* Patrick's syndicated humorous advice column Dear Cthulhu has been collected in *Have A Dark Day, Good Advice For Bad People,* and *Cthulhu Knows Best.* A number of his books are part of the set and props department at the CSI television show and have been spotted on the show. His urban fantasy *Fairy With A Gun* has been optioned by Laurence Fishburne's Cinema Gypsy Productions for film and TV. Drop by www.patthomas.net to learn more or find out about The Patrick Thomas Show mockumentary.

Originating from the UK but now residing in the Canary Islands, **Teresa Tunaley** finds more time to devote to her love of art and writing. For more than 30 years she has been doodling traditionally with pencils and dabbling with watercolors.

Along with published stories and poetry, she can be credited with award winning cover art and illustrations for author stories. Her work can be seen online and in print across the UK, US, Canada and Europe.

"I like to think that I am very versatile in my choice of subject matter—my new surroundings provide the inspiration for me to paint on a daily basis and the fact that others may enjoy my work gives me the confidence to continue."

Louise Webster graduated Magna Cum Laude with a degree in Communication Arts. Immediately after college, she wrote the evening news for a small cable TV company.

Staying home to raise her children afforded her the opportunity to write poetry for many of the small presses. She has also written an article for a psychology book, a horticulture magazine and won a contest on the history of Lake Ronkonkoma.

Louise has had poetry accepted by June Cotner for two of her anthologies, *Dog Blessings* and *House Blessings*. She had a short story published in *Nurturing Paws* edited by Lynn C. Johnston.

Most recently, her poetry has been accepted by *Tales of the Talisman*, edited by David Lee Summers.

Neil Weston lives in the UK. He has been published in such diverse publications as *Big Pulp*, *Space and Time Magazine*, the *Futuredaze* Anthology, *Disturbed Digest*, *Outposts of Beyond*, *Bloodbond*, *Scifaikuest*, *Mobius: the journal for social change*, *Eye to the Telescope* and earlier editions of *Tales of the Talisman*.

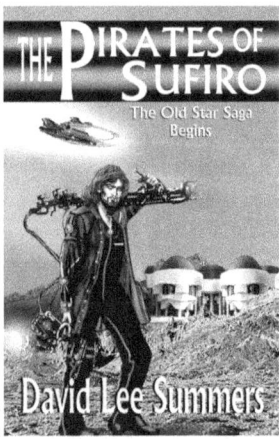

www.ingramcontent.com/pod-product-compliance
Lightning Source LLC
Chambersburg PA
CBHW080752120626
46557CB00005B/1241